Sorceress Valkyrie

OPHELIA KEE

OPHELIA KEE

Cover Design by Ophelia Kee

Copyright © 2024 by Ophelia Kee

All rights reserved.

No portion of this book may be reproduced in any form without written permission from the publisher or author, except as permitted by U.S. copyright law.

*For the love of Fated Mates
and Fantasy Adventures*

Introduction to Draoithe

Draoithe Saga

Steamy hot, wickedly delicious paranormal romance, magical realism, and urban fantasy stories set in a dream to live for!

Those who come to Draoithe aid in the fight to restore the magical balance of the dream, one couple at a time.

Grab a good drink, curl up in a good seat, choose a book from the Saga, and escape into the dream while you meet the men and women who call it home.

Draoithe is a world in which myths, legends, and fairytales walk among the strange and wonderful.

They often find balance in a lifemate, and the magic from the past lives again!

Welcome to the dream...

Steamy Urban Fantasy and Paranormal Romance Stories with Fated Mates 18+ HEA! NC!

***Warning: Adult Themes, Fantasy Violence, and/or Explicit Sexual Situations. Intended for a Mature Audience.

A Note from Ophelia Kee

Note to the Reader:
A saga is defined as a long story of heroic achievement, especially a medieval prose narrative often found in Old Norse or Old Icelandic. It's a form of the novel in which the members of a social group chronicle a long story detailing a dramatic history.

Compartmentalized in several miniseries for easier reading, the Draoithe Saga tells the story of the founding of an immortal kingdom in the Leaindeail to combat those responsible for unbalancing the magic of the dream. It's told through the eyes of those connected with its creation and the readers see the story through tales of couples who find hope through their connection to Draoithe.

The central time frame is the year 2016, although pertinent information from the past reveals itself as the characters understand it. The central place is an eerily familiar yet magical realist, Tyler, Texas. As the tale draws out, other kingdoms set in other locations interact with the Druid pack to bring about the end of Peter Elliot and restore the balance of magic, so those tales, too, became a part of the Draoithe Saga as well. Cameo appearances of characters from other tales are common. Overlapping scenes from the events often relates alternate perspectives as the story unfolds.

Watch the trailer, research videos, vlogs, and more on YouTube.

Subscribe to Ophelia Kee on YouTube

Story Description

Sorceress Valkyrie
Valkyrie Riders Volume 5
A Draoithe Saga Tale
Light magic conquers dark magic

As her attraction to Blaze deepens, Grace slowly embraces her new life at Draoithe. Her fear holds her back from accepting Blaze's offer to become his Valkyrie, but the magic he offers intrigues her, and like a moth to a flame, the sorceress desires to command his dark magic herself.

Blaze lacks the proper social skills to woo the woman he desires for his Valkyrie, so he determines to more than make up for his deficits by providing for her, protecting her, and offering her a dragon's set of skills in the bedroom. Blaze gets one grand opportunity to prove himself to her and give her the peace of mind she needs when Luke orders him to serve as the bodyguard to his newly hired jeweler. If he can convince Grace to trade her fears for his strength, he may yet win his Valkyrie.

Sorceress Valkyrie is the fifth volume in the Valkyrie Riders miniseries and part of the Draoithe Saga by Ophelia Kee. In this dark urban fantasy, light and dark magic clash as a forbidden romance blooms. As the magic continues to call to those who could aid Luke's efforts to rebalance its magic,

Grace can choose the security Blaze offers, or allow her fears to force her away from everything a dragon has to give.

It's more than a story; it's an experience. Welcome to the dream...

Urban Fantasy and Steamy Paranormal Romance with Fated Mates 18+ HEA! NC!

***Warning: Adult Themes, Fantasy Violence, and/or Explicit Sexual Situations. Intended for a Mature Audience.

Character Introduction

Meet the Characters from Dungeon Master and Sorceress Valkyrie

Lachlain Erskine,
Blaze

Blaze was once the Dungeon Master for the king of Leinster. The dark streak which allowed him to torture his enemies remains, but his meanness extends only to those who seek to harm the ones he loves. When he finds his life mate dying, he bleeds for her and stops her from crossing over, but she is a sorceress and his magic isn't good for her. It takes a bit to convince the hesitant jeweler that Blaze really is the dragon he says he is, but when he finally does, sparks fly.

Lachlain Erskine
AKA Blaze
Smells like: Juniper and whiskey
Stocks and Investments
Called by Andrei
Mate: Grace
Blue black hair
Ebony eyes
6'5" tall
245 lbs
629 years old
Grey Dragon-Alpha

Blaze is the banker. Occasionally his skills as a dungeon master get put to the test. To be a free dragon at Draoithe, he is more than willing to put the enemy to the question, even if Draoithe technically has no dungeon.

Grace Jenkins, Sorceress

Jewel is a sorcerer and a jeweler. She was doing all right running her small time jewelry and gift store in Waco, until three evil dragons came calling, ripped off her merchandise, burned down her business and kidnapped her for some crazy evil medical experiment. She had given up hope and faded. Her last memory of a handsome man was what she would take into the underworld until she woke trapped in her own mind to discover the man was a dragon who bled for her so he could claim her as his Valkyrie.

Grace Jenkins
AKA Jewel
Smells like: Jasmine

Jeweler of Miser's Touch
Mate: Blaze
Platinum Blonde hair
Pale green eyes
5'5" tall
135 lbs
330 yrs old
Valkyrie-Sorceress submissive

Grace Jenkins discovers Draoithe is truly a sanctuary when she realizes the police of the Domhain consider her a fugitive arsonist and blame her for losing her business. Blaze becomes her knight in dark armor when he offers to give her everything he has ever hoarded to ease her suffering when she realizes she has lost it all.

Contents

Newsletter Friends		XVII
1. Homemade		1
2. Ledger Book		8
3. Marked		16
4. Using His Magic		21
5. Light Magic		31
6. Wouldn't Look Good		37
7. Just As He Said		44
8. Dragon Look Bad		50
9. As Badly As		56
10. Jewel Groaned		62

11.	Out Of The Question	68
12.	Throw The Match	74
13.	Headed For	81
14.	Begging For Him	87
15.	Join The Pack	93
16.	A Little Hesitant	99
17.	Who Served	105
18.	As He Had Said	111
19.	Juniper And Whiskey	119
Epilogue		124
A Sneak Peek at Dark Curse		129
Want More From The Dream?		138
Also by Ophelia Kee		142
Acknowledgments		145
Contact Ophelia Kee		146
About the Author - Ophelia Kee		147

Newsletter Friends

Magic Scroll

Dear Reader,
Sorceress Valkyrie is Volume 5
in the Valkyrie Riders Miniseries.
I hope you enjoy it all.
For more information,
please join my group of
Newsletter Friends

Newsletter Friends

Welcome to the dream...

CHAPTER ONE

Homemade

Grace

"Did you choose one?" Blaze asked.

"Choose one what?"

Was he asking if she'd chosen a lover?

"Quarters? Upstairs or down?"

"I'm to live here?!"

The place was huge, the quarters massive. She thought they were for the guests.

"This house is for pack members. The guests will all stay at the hotel or have private quarters in the forest along trails leading back to the hotel, the stables, the parking garage, the entertainment area, and the farm."

"I would live here? This was what Luke meant by room and board?"

Grace stood still, overwhelmed. Blaze nodded.

The rooms were beautiful, and the lavatories finishes were tile, marble, and granite. The living area and bedroom spaces had hardwood floors, and all the rooms included soundproofing and light-proofing, shutters, air conditioning, lights, and ceiling fans, which all had computer controls. It was too fancy.

"Where do you stay?"

Grace needed to know where Blaze would be. Would he be close?

"It depends on which quarters you choose. You had me written into your employment contract. My orders are to serve as your protection. I'll stay wherever you do."

Grace blew out the breath she hadn't realized she held. She needed him to keep the nightmares away and to keep her safe.

As long as he stayed with her, everything seemed okay. She didn't think about her recent ordeal. He made it seem as if it were someone else's problem.

"If you would prefer, I can discuss it with Luke, and you can have your personal space. I don't want to make you uncomfortable."

Blaze offered her something she adamantly didn't want.

"No! Absolutely not. Look, I don't understand this lifemate shifter thing, but you make me feel safe. If I sleep with you, I don't think about what happened. I smell juniper and whiskey, and I can sleep. I don't know how long it will take for me to close my eyes and not see that place or those men, but until it happens, I don't want to give up the one thing which has made it possible for me to deal with a living nightmare."

Grace cried, and Blaze had her in his arms immediately.

He held her and talked low to her. He stroked her back and let her hold him tight. She breathed in his scent of *juniper and whiskey,* and the dream slowly righted itself for her.

"I'll stay and do whatever it takes for as long as it takes, even if it means I stay forever. I don't have anywhere else to be."

He tried to soothe her.

"Blaze, I need you. I know you say otherwise, but I feel as if I'm imposing on your life. I'm sorry you somehow got roped into being my caretaker."

Grace sniffed at him.

"Jewel, you haven't roped me into anything. You aren't imposing on my life. You are my life. I came here because I knew I'd find you here. Everything I've done since I arrived connects to finding you, helping you, or claiming you for mine. You can't apologize to me for my choices."

Blaze was too much. He was too kind.

Grace had lost everything. She had nothing to offer him, and yet he had willingly gifted her with everything he had, even if she told him to go away.

Blaze wanted to stay with her, care for her, provide for her, and protect her. He was attractive to her. Could a sorceress have a dragon lover?

"Why me? Why choose a broken woman with nothing left to offer you?"

"Grace, I don't need material possessions from you. I don't care if you're broken. So am I. I don't know why it's you, but it's you. You're the only one in the dream who can give me what I need. If there is even a slim chance I can have it from you, I'll do whatever it takes to convince you I'm right, and you're to be my Valkyrie."

"Okay, let's go see the rest of the mansion."

She needed time to think.

They toured the office spaces and the enormous conference room. The entire place was magnificent. To be living and working at Draoithe excited Grace.

The future no longer looked so dim. It was a bright prospect, but it paled in comparison with Blaze. Somehow, amidst all the splendor and beauty of Draoithe, her dark, serious dragon was slowly drawing her in like a magnet.

"Blaze, could you prove it to me? I mean, is there a way for me to know I'm the lifemate you think I am?"

She needed to know.

"There is, but I doubt you'd be ready for the traditional method for proving a lifemate."

Blaze answered as they left the house and walked out to the garage.

"What is it?"

"A true shifter lifemate-pair can link their emotions together during sex if they refuse to look away from one another until they both climax. If they're mates, the link will open in the mind like a candle flame, allowing the linked pair to feel what each other feels. It's usually done when a shifter determines a human who would need to be turned is their partner. It's proof."

Blaze explained it all in the third person. Grace appreciated him not creating a mental image of the two of them trying it. She suspected he'd explained it that way for both of them. He wasn't comfortable with his desire for her because she wasn't ready. It only added to her attraction to him.

"If the link worked, how would a dragon's mate become a Valkyrie?"

She needed to know the details.

"It's part of the shifter bonding ritual. A dragon bites his mate and drinks from her, starting the bond. A dragon's bite is painful, but it turns their mate, giving them the ability to use the dragon's magic. His mate has to bite him back and drink from him. Sharing blood allows the magic to ignite. When a dragon enters his mate and touches her center, his blood grants her wings and fangs. The magic forces both parties to climax, and it demands a lot of energy to merge the souls in the bond. It's often a lengthy and violent encounter. To seal the bond, both parties have to drink from one another at the end. The dragon's mate drinks her fill to allow her to use his magic completely. The dragon drinking his mate's blood seals him to her as his only rider. A bonded dragon has only one rider, and she alone can command her dragon to serve her."

They walked around and saw the stables and the two draft horses Kallik worked with every morning. They saw the nearly finished university, library, art gallery, and sound stage. Javier caught up with them before five and explained where some other buildings would be and how the horseback riding trails would work.

It would be a resort-like property after the construction. She had an idea where her shop would be, where she would learn the staff, and where she would practice her magic. She could almost see her new life.

Grace looked at Blaze. She still wasn't sure how he fit in the vision, but it would feel wrong if he weren't in it. No matter how she might like to refuse it, Blaze had become an integral part of her life.

Grace nodded to herself. It would be upstairs. No more dark dungeons for Blaze. He'd lived in the dungeons long enough.

Javier promised to lock up before he went back to Fox's house, and Blaze took Grace to the coolest store, which was a restaurant when they left the retreat build-site. They had ice cream at a place called Braum's. It was homemade.

CHAPTER TWO

Ledger Book

Luke

He slipped out of the room while Eli napped. He wanted to convince her to retire from her career as a high school teacher. Since she'd gone to summer break, she had more energy, and it had spelled more sex, which he seemed to want more than ever.

After he had loaned the Mustang to Blaze, Eli had cornered him in the room and taken her pleasure from him for two hours. He had no complaints.

He had claw marks down his back, making his shirt uncomfortable, and his legs had a delicious jelly feeling. But he loved it.

Never in his wildest imagination had he dreamed he would find his mate in a tiger. Eli was more than Luke deserved, but he wasn't about to give up his kitty cat.

Remembering had him grinning. He'd gone to look for the ledger he'd left on the nightstand. She'd been waiting for him. When he walked into the room, the door had clicked and then locked. When he turned, Eli stood in front of it, blocking his exit, and he found he had no desire to leave.

Damn, the woman was sexy. He had to have more shirts made. Half the buttons were missing from the one he'd been wearing.

She had bitten him, drank from him, and marked him again. He had tiger fang marks on both sides of his throat. Her scent marked him so heavily he smelled of *shade in the summer*. He was her territory, and it felt amazing.

Luke rolled the sleeves on his shirt as he moved down the hall toward the study with the missing ledger under his arm. It finally hit him why he'd been so spectacularly used by his tiger today.

He'd interviewed the women they'd rescued for the past few days. None of them had bonded. It was Eli's idea, but her tiger didn't care. It wanted the entire known universe to know Luke belonged to her.

He'd run into Blaze and Grace looking to borrow a vehicle. It was the smell of *jasmine* which had made Eli's nose wrinkle. She smelled it on his hand from where they had shaken hands earlier and faintly on his clothes from the encounter in the garage.

He wanted to kiss Eli, to reassure her. But he caught his bottom lip on her fang, and she tasted him. Her normal possessiveness made her territorial as always, but smelling the unbonded sorceress' scent on him sent her over the edge.

She ripped his shirt off and bit him immediately, marking him by chewing into his throat as she drank from him. She pushed him onto the bed while his head swam with euphoria and took his cock out of his pants and mounted him. Her claws had sunk into his pectoral muscles, holding him in place so she could use him.

Eli rode him roughly until she came, but she refused to let him up. She shifted positions and sank back onto his cock, slowly letting it fill her asshole. She fucked his cock up her ass until she climaxed again.

She was done with him. He was still hard.

When she removed her claws, releasing him, he flipped her onto her back and finished himself coming in her ass as her claws raked down his sides and back.

Luke probably looked like he had been in a fight, but he didn't care. How many men got mauled by a possessive tiger for their afternoon delight? His guess was few, and they were all probably as stupidly happy as he was.

He bumped into Ryker, headed for the garage as he finished rolling the second sleeve. He hadn't buttoned the top three buttons on his shirt. His neck was too sore for it.

Ryker clapped him on the shoulder, and Luke winced. Ryker's smile of greeting turned into concern. He looked at him closely then.

"Did I miss a fight?"

Luke laughed.

"No. I made the mistake of encountering Eli in a frisky mood, with the smell of *jasmine* still on my hand."

"Eli did that to you?"

"Tigers are extremely possessive and highly territorial. I swear, I'm seriously tempted to shake hands with as many unbonded women as humanly possible from now on."

Luke grinned.

"That good, hunh?"

Ryker laughed.

"Hell yeah. When you grabbed my shoulder, I thought about going back for seconds. When I bumped into you, I was daydreaming about how many men could say they got mauled by a possessive tiger for an afternoon delight."

"I don't think there are many, but I hope they're all as crazy happy as you seem to be."

"Hey, I loaned the Mustang to Blaze earlier. It was in the driveway, and I wasn't sure what you worked on otherwise."

"Okay, I'll watch for him. Sorry, I'm late."

"I thought you were early. I wasn't expecting you until sunset. The last time I checked, you were a vampire."

His old lieutenant remained uncomfortable with not having a 'reporting for duty' hour.

"Yeah, about that. Have you got a minute? I wanted to show you something."

Luke decided the ledger could wait a little longer. Ryker had been his friend too long for Luke not to be concerned by the tone in the man's voice.

"Sure man, what's up?"

"I think it's easier if I show you than explain it. Come with me."

Ryker ducked into the garage. Luke followed him.

Ryker stood in front of the door to the driveway. He nodded to Luke.

"Open it," Ryker instructed.

"Are you crazy?!"

The sun fried vampires into crispy ashes. They had almost lost Ryker once. Was Ryker ill? Had he developed depression? Was he suicidal? Lily had bitten him. He hadn't given his consent to the panther who turned him into a shifter.

"Just do it."

The man didn't act depressed.

Luke still had his eyebrows raised. Lily would maul him for real if Ryker became dust in the breeze. Luke opened the door.

Ryker stood there and let the sun touch him. Nothing happened. No smoke, no ashes, no dead and gone vampire. What the hell was that about?

"What's going on?"

"I don't know exactly, but it feels weird. Like I'm too warm, but it's much easier than it was two days ago when it first happened. It feels like the shifter magic is protecting me somehow. I feel the panther close to the surface when the light touches me."

Ryker frowned. Luke closed the door. He studied his old friend, waiting for him to finish speaking.

"Luke, last night I accidentally swallowed food. It didn't stay down. I won't lie. It's a little frightening. I was okay with being a vampire. I'm a little afraid of not being one," Ryker admitted.

"I wouldn't stop drinking from your source. Shifter magic is more powerful than vampire magic, but you only have a small amount. When a shifter becomes immortal, it takes about a month before the magic grows to its full potential. I'm not an expert, but you became zduhaci. Andrei and Mihaela both assured me you had full strength and total use of your vampire magic when you woke up, even if you lacked skills. I don't think there are take backs. Tolerance to the sun and eventually eating some food may be a side effect of the increasing shifter magic. But you'll always be a vampire."

Luke told him the truth as far as he understood it. Lily hadn't meant to turn him. It had been an accident Ryker could shift at all. He seemed happy with his strange immortality.

He wasn't happy at all about potentially losing part of it. If Luke had to guess, Ryker probably feared losing the vampire allure more than anything else. He'd used it to save both Lily and Artie.

"Maybe you'll get lucky and be a day walking panther vampire."

Luke grinned.

"It would be alright as long as I don't have to give up anything. I could be fine with it."

Ryker seemed a bit more hopeful and less concerned, but Ryker had always lived his life as it came at him. He rarely worried about the future much. Luke left Ryker working on installing the light-blocking drapes in a Hummer and carried the ledger book back to his office.

CHAPTER THREE

Marked

L^{uke}

He threw the ledger on the desk in his office and stepped out into the late afternoon sunlight. He could look over the list of business expenses again later. Luke wanted to ensure they spent their money wisely, but it wasn't as if he was in any jeopardy of running out of money, not since the dragons arrived.

He soaked up the sun and enjoyed the feel of healing tiger claw marks when the Mustang rolled back into the driveway. Blaze got out of the car and immediately went around to help Grace.

The dragons were formal, old-school, gentlemanly-types with women. It balanced their more vicious dark side in policing the realm.

Fox had been right about them. They were good men. If he could get past all the etiquette rules they followed, he thought he'd enjoy friendships with dragons.

Blaze approached him to return the keys. He hissed rather evilly when he saw Luke up close.

"My king, what happened? Why was I not called?"

"I don't normally invite dragons into my bedroom, Blaze. One tiger is quite enough for me, I assure you."

Luke grinned.

Blaze quirked an eyebrow, then grinned at him. He was a different man when he grinned. Blaze was serious-minded, but Luke liked him. He knew in his gut the stoic dragon was worth getting to know.

"I can see where you'd think a dragon was too much in that arena."

Blaze laughed. It was dark with implied humor.

It was good to know something amused. He appeared to loosen up. The dark streak which ran through Blaze was still there, but it felt less sinister when the dragon relaxed.

Luke wouldn't want to be the man's enemy, though. Of all the dragons, Blaze felt the darkest.

"Do you require healing?" Grace asked.

"No. Absolutely not!"

Luke wasn't about to let Grace touch him. At least, not until he was less lacerated. Then he might consider it because it could get his tiger in the mood to lacerate him again.

"Jewel, I fear you may be the reason for his current appearance. You best not."

Blaze tried to explain. Grace stared at him with a confused frown.

"Grace, Eli's a tiger shifter. Tigers are extremely territorial. We shook hands earlier. Eli felt she needed to mark me as hers again. I'm fine. I rather like being the property of a possessive tiger."

Luke explained the situation with a smile.

Then he returned his attention to Blaze before the dragon grew aggravated with Luke for paying too much attention to his unbonded mate. Grace needed time to become accustomed to the people at Draoithe and not being a shifter made it a little harder to understand.

Some women might find his current appearance hard to accept. Some immortals who were unfamiliar with the shifter world didn't get it immediately.

Considering how good he felt at the moment, he wasn't about to hide that aspect of his life, however. His tiger marked him, and he liked it. The non-shifter immortals would simply need to learn.

"Did you like the car?"

"Nice set of wheels. I enjoyed driving it. We only dented one bumper."

"You dented the bumper? How the hell did you do that?" Luke asked.

"Not really."

Blaze grinned, tossing Luke the keys.

"It drove great. I filled up the tank for you. Thanks for loaning it to us."

"Eli likes the car. If you'd dented it, I might have needed healing."

Luke laughed.

Blaze was getting better. It was good to see him happy. Grace must have done something good for him. Maybe the dragons could work things out and claim their Valkyries the way everyone else seemed to claim their mates. Things might work out for everyone better than he hoped.

He pushed the niggling questions about the strange coincidences concerning mates to the back of his mind. It seemed less important than taking care of his men, as he'd always done. So he stayed focused on Blaze and Grace.

"Can we expect you for twilight dinner tonight?"

Blaze looked at Grace, who nodded. Blaze answered for them.

"I think so. Thanks again."

They grasped their forearms. The ancient greeting felt as good with the dragons as it did with Fox or Ryker. He had a force to reckon with. Eli had greater safety. The situation pleased the direwolf.

Dinner later was great. Eli blushed prettily at Luke's appearance, and most of the guys laughed. It was an amusement because he'd found so much joy in playing with a tiger.

Javier looked at Luke, then looked at Eli, grinning.

"I always knew territorialism was better than jealousy."

Luke grinned back at his beta. Javier looked jealous because his phoenix hadn't marked him similarly.

CHAPTER FOUR
Using His Magic

A ndrei

When he and Nadine returned from flying around eleven, Nadine continued to catalog all the information Fox and Artie had collected over about four centuries of researching immortals.

Normally, he would have practiced with his staff, then showered and helped Nadine until right before dawn, but Andrei saw Blaze sitting in the gazebo. His laptop lay open, but he sat, lost in thought, and he had long forgotten whatever he intended to work on.

Andrei liked the dragon. He, too, it seemed, had spent a long time serving others and hiding his true self. Nadine alone knew the man Andrei was. Andrei suspected no one knew the real Blaze.

When he was sure Nadine was safely back inside the house, he walked over to the dragon, whose purpose at Draoithe was to protect Andrei's stake in it.

"Can't sleep?"

Andrei stepped into the gazebo.

Blaze rose to his feet and bowed.

"My king, how may I serve?"

Blaze responded with entirely too much etiquette.

Andrei wanted to laugh at how proper Blaze sounded, but two months earlier, at the enclave, he probably sounded just as proper. Instead, he pointed out the facts of his situation to yet another dragon.

"Blaze, please call me Andrei, or if you prefer Fangs. But I must tell you I'm not truly a king. Two months ago, I was the personal guard to the vjestice Princess of the now lost Cioaran Enclave. I only stopped to see if I might assist you somehow."

"Fangs, I should work, but I admit my head is somewhere else. I'm sorry if I have bothered you."

"You didn't bother me, simply getting me out of staff practice. Nadine and I returned from flying. Usually, I practice, but I saw you and detoured."

"You practice with the staff, too?"

"Yeah, do you need a sparring partner? Sometimes it helps to clear your mind."

Andrei grew curious about the dragon's abilities. It had been a long time since he had a new challenger, and at Draoithe, he might have found more in the dragons. Maybe he hadn't gotten out of staff practice after all.

"Grace is asleep. I don't wish to disturb her, and I seem to be overdressed for staves."

"I can help with the clothes issue if you like. You wait here. I'll be right back."

He winked out of the gazebo and into the laundry room. He grabbed a pair of extra-large joggers, then winked into his room and grabbed two staves. Another wink and he stood in front of Blaze in the gazebo, handing the man some pants. Teleportation made life easier.

"Here. Get changed. We can practice the moves on the patio."

Blaze grinned and nodded. The man stripped off his clothes with the ease of long practice. He was a shifter. Andrei shed his shirt and shoes, and the two men walked barefoot over the damp grass to the deck.

"Is it big enough?"

"I once kicked Fox's ass on this deck."

"Then it will do."

They both took stances and moved through basic forms. Blaze was smooth. He had probably mastered the staff centuries ago. Andrei let the allure swell slowly.

"So, let me guess. Grace stops you from getting work done. Am I right?"

Incredibly, Blaze opened up a little and answered him. It might be easier than Andrei thought.

"Yeah, I think I may have made a mistake."

"How so?"

"She asked me a lot of questions about shifters, and I answered her. Grace is immortal, but she knows little about shifters and their quirks. The dragon in me wants to deny her nothing."

"I don't see how you made a mistake yet."

The staff spun around and connected with Andrei's palm. He let his allure intensify slightly. He wanted to keep the taciturn dragon talking.

"Well, the questions got serious and slightly personal. She asked me how a dragon turns their mate into a Valkyrie, then she asked me for a way to prove to her she was mine. I told her how. I think it may have been a mistake."

"Not following you. What option did you have? The truth always works best. Nadine asked me to link with her first, so she would know if I was her mate. Fear consumed me. I had already lost myself to her. If it hadn't worked, I might have walked into the sun, but I understood why she needed it. I mean, I'm a vampire."

Cool rain in the moonlight filled the night air as Andrei worked up a sweat with the rhythm of a more advanced kata.

Blaze slid through the end of the kata he practiced and rested the staff on the floor. He took up another stance to practice a different series of moves. He was good. Andrei hoped he got the chance to spar with the man sometime.

"I hadn't looked at it from that perspective. You might be right. Reassurance for her could be good. I was more concerned I had pressured her into what I wanted, as opposed to letting her decide. I don't want that, and I doubt she's even close to a decision involving a lover, much less a lifemate."

"Then drag it out. You could always formalize your courtship, or you could deliberately create space in the relationship, so she knows your interest but doesn't feel pressured. Choose to let her make the advances."

"Honestly, I fear formalizing the courtship. I don't wish for her to have any other suitors. Truthfully, the dragon in me wishes to incinerate any man who gets too close to her. This morning, I almost killed her servant because she ran into him while toweling her hair. He touched her, and I nearly lost my mind."

Blaze shook his head, but his form stayed perfect. He had practiced katas for many years. Staves were excellent focus sticks.

"She's a powerful sorceress, but she's not an alpha. Submissives rarely start any advances. I have tried to put the space in the relationship, as you say, but she keeps manipulating the situation to remove it."

"What do you mean, she's manipulating the situation?"

He kept his tone deliberately mild and appeared to all who might look as if focused on his staff and only casually conversing with Blaze.

"She died, and I had to bleed for her. She's my mate. I got all dragon defensive, and even my brothers didn't interfere for almost a whole day. They feared to rile the dragon in me. I tried to let her sleep alone when she finally escaped the dream trap my blood induced, but she begged me to sleep with her, and I couldn't say 'no' because I'm a dragon. I serve."

Blaze talked as the staff moved.

"Today, when Luke offered to rebuild her jewelry business at Draoithe, she negotiated with him to order me to be her bodyguard. I think she tricked me into giving her all the information on shifter mating rituals somehow."

Andrei had a million questions, but they'd have to wait. Blaze needed a sounding board, not a student.

"You give her too much credit. I doubt she played you. Perhaps you're paranoid and have over thought it all. She probably feels safe with you because you rescued her and protected her. Her most recent experience with men was all bad. It's not like she's made advances toward you."

Andrei left space for Blaze to either continue or change the subject.

"No. I kissed her. I shouldn't have done it, either. She wasn't ready, and I knew it. But she pressed me, and well, I'm a dragon. She didn't understand, but I should never have allowed things to devolve to that level."

Ah, finally the heart of the matter. He felt guilty for kissing the woman he desired, and he feared she viewed him as lesser because he was weak for her and gave in to his desire.

Blaze had gotten focused on himself. What he needed was to focus on Grace.

"Did she run away after you kissed her?"

"No, she asked me if I had kissed other women. When I told her 'no', she asked me not to kiss anyone else. I want nothing but her."

Blaze admitted his singular, all-consuming desire.

"Sounds to me as if she enjoyed kissing you. She staked a claim on you, and she expects you to wait for her. I think you're focused on the wrong issues, my friend."

Blaze cocked an eyebrow up for him to continue.

"She's probably subconsciously ensured an opportunity to learn about you without taking a chance that you'll disappear if she takes a long time or you turn out to be a monster like the men at the warehouse. She's not a shifter, so she plays the game differently. I think you should link with her when she demands her proof. You already know how to make it happen without sex. If she needs it, you won't deny her."

Blaze froze. He blinked. He looked at the staff in his outstretched hand, then looked at Andrei for a long minute. It finally occurred to him Andrei had made himself into the sounding board Blaze needed to see the truth. He was too involved to see it clearly on his own.

"How did you do that, Fangs?"

Blaze's tone held surprise and suspicion.

"Years of practice dealing with a closed-off princess who desperately needed a friend. Oh, and did I forget to mention I'm a vampire? No, I'm positive I mentioned it. Staves are the best of weapons, don't you agree?"

Andrei smiled. He knew grey dragons couldn't use iron weapons.

"Indeed. I think I have to agree. Thank you, Fangs. I needed a sounding board. Do you always practice now, or did you say it to help me?"

"I always practice now. Lying is dishonorable, my friend. I was also serious about sparring. If you like, I would love to have a go at a dragon. I think I'm pretty good. Are you interested?"

He could use a good sparring partner. He needed to waste some energy. Fox hadn't been available lately.

"I'll meet you tomorrow. May I borrow your staff? I brought only my spear. It's good for a true battle, but..."

"Keep it. Fox has like fifty for practice. He won't mind. Tomorrow at eleven, then?"

"Tomorrow at eleven."

Blaze grasped right forearms with Andrei, gathered his clothes and shoes, and left. Andrei winked into the bathroom for a shower before joining Nadine to continue their work. It felt right, using his magic to help Blaze.

CHAPTER FIVE
Light Magic

Grace

She woke up alone, afraid, and slightly confused about where she was. Then the smell of *juniper and whiskey* came to her, and she calmed. She heard the typing on the keyboard as he worked on something on his laptop.

His black hair was damp, and he sat in a chair farther from the bed. His towel from the shower lay over the back of the other chair. He drank straight whiskey from a glass next to him on the table.

Dressed only in his boxers, she studied him for a minute before he felt her eyes on him. He glanced up at her, smiled, and looked back at the screen.

He typed something more, then reached blindly for his whiskey. He took a long sip while he read something, set the glass back down, and typed again.

Grace watched Blaze work for several long moments. She studied the dragon tattoo on his pectoral muscle just above his heart as his fingers danced over the keyboard.

She had never liked tattoos, but someone had tastefully rendered his ink. She wondered what it would feel like to trace over it with her fingers. Would his smooth skin feel like satin stretched over stone? The way it looked?

"Do you like what you see, Jewel?"

She'd been staring for a while. Grace averted her eyes, but not before she saw the hint of a smile play over his face.

"Sorry, I thought you were a dream."

What else could she say? She dreamed of him before she woke up. It was almost the truth.

"Am I a pleasant dream or a nightmare?"

The hint of a smile faded. He almost held his breath, hoping she didn't say nightmare.

"A pleasant dream."

She rubbed her eyes.

"How so?"

He continued working.

Still sleepy-headed, she answered the truth without thinking first.

"You kissed me again."

Blaze's fingers froze on the keyboard.

"If kissing me is a pleasant dream, what's the nightmare?"

His eyes remained on the screen. He asked, but feared her response.

"Losing you."

Grace sat on the edge of the bed. Blaze asked if she needed anything.

"What time is it?"

Should get up and start her day or go back to sleep.

"It's almost one-thirty in the morning."

"Do dragons not sleep?"

"Jewel, you know I sleep. You fell asleep at about ten and honestly, I needed to get some work done. I slipped out, so I didn't disturb you. But I couldn't concentrate. Fangs ran into me at the gazebo and offered to practice staves, so I could clear my head and focus. It worked. We're going to spar tomorrow at eleven. Ash will be happy. I'm about a quarter of the way finished filling in the blanks for the jewelry store's business model."

"Well, I'm awake now. Can I help?"

"Actually, yes. What are you going to name the store?"

"Miser's Touch."

It seemed appropriate.

"Do you want to sell anything besides fine jewelry?"

"Yeah, I want to sell high-end decorative items, watches, and timepieces. You know, cuckoo clocks, silver, and gold plated items like plates or mugs, and those nice jewelry boxes, too. It should be a treasure store instead of a jewelry store."

Grace thought out loud, and Blaze nodded and typed as she spoke.

"Handcrafted items, specialty items, engraving, and cleaners. You know, all the cool stuff. I need locking display cases and some open display shelving."

Grace daydreamed about what her store needed and looked like.

"Wait, hold up. I haven't gotten to that part yet. Hey, do you want a drink? I need a refill. If you're up to it, we'll sit and fill in some of this. What do you think?"

Blaze smiled at her.

He was in a good mood. She agreed. Grace straightened her clothes, which were a little rumpled. He pulled on a pair of joggers, and she went with him to the bar in the living room to refill his whiskey.

They found Flame and Hannah talking low. Hannah was a pretty lady with long red hair. Flame couldn't resist her allure, but he seemed to both recognize and enjoy it. The entire room smelled like *lavender*.

Blaze walked by, grinning, and snapped his fingers in his brother's ear. Flame scowled up at him.

"Snap out of it, bro, or you'll be there all night again. Perhaps you two should work on something else, like levitation or making ice."

Blaze laughed.

Flame nodded at Hannah when she looked at him. Hannah looked at Blaze and froze his feet while he walked. He fell forward, but caught himself as the dragon fire came out and melted his feet from the floor.

Grace laughed. She couldn't help it.

"We're working on controlling the allure. Nightshade has the flame and the ice down pat. She's gotten pretty good at levitation, and her speed will come easily when she runs. What good is any of it if her allure doesn't work, and she can't hunt?"

Flame scowled at Blaze as he refilled his whiskey. Grace shuddered at the idea of needing to drink blood to remain alive. Her magic recoiled from the darkness inherent in that idea.

"Hey, did you see the business model for the floral shop?"

"Yeah, but Ember traded me his work for the Floral Shop model. Looks like I'm helping Lightning write employment contracts for a couple of weeks."

"Makes sense."

"Jewel, what do you want to drink?"

"Do you have any wine?"

Blaze took out a glass and served her a glass of wine. Hannah lifted hers and smiled at Grace. The pretty red-haired vampire also liked red wine.

"Flame, do you want a refill? Hannah?"

Blaze took over bartending for a moment. He refilled Flame's cognac, topped off Hannah's wine, and refilled his whiskey.

"Why are you guys up so late?" Flame asked.

"Bothering you in the middle of the night."

Blaze grinned at his brother. Flame laughed.

"We're working on the business model for the jewelry store," Blaze said.

"You aren't learning any secret light magic?"

"What would a dragon do with light magic?" Blaze asked.

CHAPTER SIX
Wouldn't Look Good

Grace

"You could learn how to defend yourself for starters,"

Flame ragged on his brother a bit.

"No time, brother. I have a sparring session tomorrow at eleven. You should come, watch, learn a few things," Blaze retorted.

Grace enjoyed seeing a new side of Blaze. He was comfortable with Flame. His friendship with Flame felt old and deep.

"With who?" Flame asked.

"Fangs. We set it up earlier. We practiced together tonight. The vampire knows what he's doing. He beat Fox before. It should prove interesting," Blaze said.

"What do you say, Nightshade? Do you want to watch Fangs take out Blaze at the staves tomorrow night?" Flame stared at the pretty redhead.

Hannah looked up at Grace.

"Are you going?"

Grace looked at Blaze, who grinned.

"I think so."

"Nadine will probably be there, too. She and Andrei fly every night around ten. I have a feeling the audience will get bigger once everyone hears about it," Blaze said.

"We should set it up so we can all spar. It would be excellent entertainment and practice. I bet Fox would be down for it and Smoke too. Let me talk to the rest of the dragons. Thursday night staves. Do you think we could get a staff for the rest of us?"

Flame was dead serious. He was a true competitor.

"Fangs said Fox has maybe fifty practice staves. I'm sure we could borrow some until our storage units ship over."

Blaze sipped his whiskey.

Grace watched curiously as he seemed to listen to something, but no one spoke.

***

Blaze

Thursday nights at eleven at night stave competitions. Fangs and Blaze are up tomorrow. Who wants in on the next one?

Flame opened the link.

I'm down. Let me sleep.

Ash yawned.

Hell yeah, sign me up. I'm putting Fox on the list, too.

Smoke chimed in.

I'm in.

Char added himself.

Ditto, but somebody needs to loan me a staff.

Lightning queried.

I'm in. Prepare yourselves to lose brothers.

Ember teased.

"Okay, eleven of us so far. We'll ask the Ruiri tomorrow," Flame said.

Blaze, it's Luke. Javier, Ryker, and I all want in. No king shit. Just stave rules.

"No, add Luke, Javier, and Ryker. He said stave rules. No going easy on anyone because they are Ruiri," Blaze said.

Flame grinned.

Blaze. It's Kallik. Griz and I want in too, but we want to watch for a while first, pencil us in for later so we can practice more first. Fox, do we have enough staves?

"Add Kallik and Griz too, but pencil them in later. They need to practice first. Hold on. Kallik is checking with Fox to see if we have enough staves for everybody," Blaze said.

I've got about sixty practice staves. We can replace any that might get broken. Come by tomorrow and pick your poison, gentleman.

"Fox says to go by tomorrow and pick your poison. He has about sixty to choose from. Set it up, Flame."

Blaze grinned.

*****

Grace

How did he know? The two men grew still and seemed to concentrate inward. Intrigue filled Grace.

"Blaze, how do you know all of that?"

Grace had to ask. It was strange. Hannah looked curious, too.

"My brothers and I are all collared together, so we can open the link and communicate telepathically with each other. One of us is with one or more of the Ruiri. Fox can use druid magic to enter any mind. Luke, Kallik, and Griz all can dreamtalk to anyone they know personally. It turns out we were all close enough to one another and the use of cell phones was unnecessary."

"You mean your brothers can all see inside your mind?"

Hannah looked horrified.

"Only when I choose, and only what I choose."

Flame calmed Hannah.

Blaze served everyone another round of drinks. Grace and Blaze took their leave of Flame and Hannah as they returned to practice, increasing and decreasing Hannah's allure. *Lavender* slowly overpowered the living room again.

"Hannah is new to her magic. How does Flame know so much about vampires?" Grace asked.

"Hannah became a vjestice vampire, but they shipped her to the warehouse we rescued you from without knowing how to use any of her magic. Flame once turned a few of his riders with magic, so he didn't have to give them up. He kept them for a while, but eventually, he got caught, and they faced the sun as a warning to dragons not to turn riders into vjestice vampires."

Blaze sighed.

"The king executed Flame and left him until dawn so he couldn't save them. I had to tell him what happened later, after he lost his mind looking for them. He'd lost about a week and a half's worth of memories in the Netherworld. It was hard on him. Later, he spent centuries studying vampires and learning everything there is to know about them. He worked for an enclave for a while and even saved a red dragon from a different enclave once."

"So if you die, you hang out in the Netherworld until you come back to yourself, but you lose memories from this realm the longer you are there?"

Grace tried to understand correctly and ignored the horror of the story Blaze explained.

"Yeah, add in the horrible part about dying and the extreme anger when we come back, and that sets it up."

"Flame's in love with Hannah, isn't he?"

"Yeah, she's his lifemate, but she's a vampire. She doesn't have to accept him. It's why he's so serious about teaching her how to hunt. He can't stand the idea she wouldn't even be able to feed herself if she left."

"Blaze, how many women did you rescue?"

Grace felt as if she had to know.

"Seven. They were all lifemates of the seven dragons who follow the Dire Wolf King. Telling you made it seem as if we all claimed it, so we could have our Valkyries all at once, but I didn't lie to you. You are my lifemate. You were all foretold to us by the necromancer who made us."

"All of you waited six centuries to find all your lifemates at the same time in that warehouse?"

Grace couldn't believe it, but Blaze was serious. He'd told her the truth, even though he knew he wouldn't look good because of it.

CHAPTER SEVEN
Just As He Said

Grace

Grace almost felt sorry for the dragons. Six hundred years was a long time to wait for a woman to not accept a dragon as her mate. Blaze had said he could prove it to her.

"Yeah, crazy I know."

They were back in the room.

"You said you could prove it to me. What if you're wrong?"

"If I'm wrong, then you run your jewelry shop at Draoithe, and I act as security for you. I would still help you any way I can, but I wouldn't pursue you, nor stand in your way from pursuing another."

"Jewel, what if I'm right? If I prove it to you, we would link. Undoing it would be impossible. If you decided you didn't wish to be my Valkyrie, I couldn't live with the loss. It's a dangerous request to ask me to prove it to you. You would need to be sure you found me acceptable and just wanted confirmation."

Blaze seemed compelled to ensure she fully understood. Grace thought she was still missing information. Blaze had a dark side. She was both terrified and thrilled by it.

She feared the entire sexual game. Could she play it anymore, after what had happened to her?

"What would it mean for me if I accepted your offer?"

Grace had to know. She liked the dragon. Blaze thrilled her. If he was right, and she got her proof, there was more to the story than her just getting wings and dark magic. She needed him to fill in the missing pieces.

"You want the potential negative aspect of being Valkyrie. Jewel, you'd be my only rider. For me to fly, we would need to have a physical relationship. The magic, which would grant you the use of my magic wouldn't allow you to deny me what I needed from you."

He didn't flinch or deny her knowledge. He would have her all the time.

"I would always have to have sex with you. That makes sense."

Grace thought she understood. Sedr magic worked because of sexual energy.

"No, Jewel. You would need to trust me, because the magic wouldn't allow you to deny me what I needed from you. The magic would interpret my desire as my need because I'd have no other means available for me to get the energy I need to fly."

Blaze reiterated his explanation.

Grace stared at him. She never wanted to be a thrall.

Grace set the wineglass down, hugged herself, and walked away from him toward the window.

It was dark outside, just as Blaze was dark. Grace was light. She was a sorceress.

Was she even seriously considering any of it? It was just a game, some fun to pass the time, right?

Who was she kidding? He had the knowledge she needed. She enjoyed flirting with the handsome, too-serious dragon. He made her feel good.

He took away the pain and fear. With him, there were no nightmares, and the memories didn't haunt her waking hours.

He was her kind man, the one who rescued her and saved her life. He was the serious dragon who rolled up his pants to walk into the creek with her, and when she pressed him, Blaze kissed her breathless and made her think she was still alive.

What if he was wrong? What if she wasn't his lifemate? It didn't seem real.

If she was his Valkyrie, he could rape her, and she couldn't stop him. She would go along with it. It would be okay for him to force himself upon her to gain the energy to fly.

That seemed like madness. Could she trust him? She didn't want to be hurt anymore.

Blaze set his whiskey down and stepped up behind her. His hands squeezed her shoulders. She ached to lean into her kind man, the one who'd saved her.

If she accepted him, things would never be the same. He would love her in ways she couldn't imagine. Part of her wanted what he offered. It thrilled her, but it also terrified her.

"Will you trust me, Grace? I've already sworn to protect you, even from myself. I can't hide it from you. But I don't give in because I can't trap you or be like the men who kidnapped you. I need you to choose me because it's what you want. I'd never hurt you. Give me the chance to prove it to you."

"You've been proving it to me since you covered me in that warehouse, and I faded. Blaze, you aren't the issue. I don't know if I'm strong enough to be the Valkyrie you need. I'm afraid of the darkness in you."

Grace was confused.

"Give me your fear, Jewel. I'll give you my strength and wait for you. I'd never force you. Instead, I promise you'd always have to come to me first. When you say you'll make the trade with me, we'll go slow, and I'll give you more than you could imagine. I can always protect you."

Blaze was so serious. It felt so right. She could believe in his promises. He hadn't lied to her, and he'd kept his word to her in everything since she first saw him.

She wanted what he offered in a way she never imagined she could. No more men taking advantage of her or using her; none taking her magic or forcing her to use sorcery for evil. Blaze would be her only lover. He'd keep her safe.

Grace nodded.

"I will trade you. The fear is too heavy for me to carry. I need your strength to move forward. I have so little of my own. Blaze, I want to go slow with you. Will you hold me while we sleep?"

"Yes, always."

Grace turned to face him. She reached up and pecked him.

"Thank you."

She whispered the words as he embraced her. He waited, just as he said he would.

CHAPTER EIGHT
Dragon Look Bad

*A*ndrei

He woke at two o'clock in the afternoon, as he usually did. Long years of rising early to meditate before he picked up his responsibilities again had made his sleep habits quite predictable, whereas his mate's sleep habits were anything but normal.

Nadine catnapped in the chair. Her laptop was on. He rose, went to her, and carefully lifted her from the chair to carry her back to the bed. He didn't wake her.

Her insomnia had improved. She often slept at least a few hours every three days. When they first met, four or five days would pass before she slept again.

She slept the longest when she slept with him, but he was a vampire. Whether he wanted it, every day at dawn he would drink from his source, make love to his eagle, and be called to sleep by the sun.

Nadine couldn't always fall asleep. They worked out a system where she worked in the room with him while he slept, so if she fell asleep, he didn't have to search for her when he woke.

It usually worked. When it failed and Nadine fell asleep somewhere else in the house, whoever found her would cover her with a blanket and leave her asleep. Andrei always went straight to her and teleported or carried her back to the room to sleep when it happened.

Whatever caused her nightmares was still a mystery, but she admitted being stalked in Seattle had made her insomnia worse because she feared the nightmare more. Andrei shielded his consort from things which might trigger her nightmares when she slept next to him.

Andrei couldn't use his allure for her with much success. She was a Philippine eagle, and he fell into her and lost himself. In a way, he was happy it didn't work well.

Nadine loved him for the man he was, not the way a vampire could make her feel. She had become his world. She was always his focus. Once his work had been all he had, but Nadine had become his *everything*.

Andrei wasn't a shifter, but he joined the pack even so. He needed society. He needed the people.

Luke was a man worth following. He not only accepted diversity, but he also seemed to prefer it.

In the Druid pack, Andrei could be himself. He could practice his magic without fear. Taking his consort had increased his abilities.

Andrei had significantly improved his skills. He took pride in his speed, and he could levitate nearly ten feet straight up. He'd been practicing the fire and ice as well against Javier's frozen phoenix flame.

His teleportation range improved nightly, and he mentally mapped locations he could teleport into. He may never again walk in the sun, but he was no longer trapped by it, either.

After meditating and organizing his thoughts, he dressed and slipped quietly from the room. He found himself in the kitchen serving himself a cup of tea when Fox found him.

"Fangs, I have to hand it to you. Thursday Night Staves has seriously taken off. There isn't a man here who isn't itching to compete."

Fox looked happy, but Andrei became lost.

"Excuse me? What are you talking about?"

"Thursdays at eleven. You and Blaze spar tonight. Lightning and Char are up next week. Flame has it all mapped out for months, and I've loaned out ten practice staves this morning already."

"I offered to spar with Blaze. When did one sparring competition turn into Thursday Night Staves?"

Andrei grinned. He liked the idea, but he couldn't take credit for it.

"About one-thirty or two in the morning last night. Javier has tried to convince Luke if it goes well, we should sell tickets to the patrons. Lightning dropped off copies of the traditional staves rules this morning when he came for another practice staff. One-hour time limit, man against man, no magic. Social standing doesn't exist."

Andrei paused, waiting to see if Fox would rub his hands together with glee. The man practically vibrated with his excitement.

"Luke's idea? That last one?"

"Yeah, he figures the dragons need to feel like accepted members of our society. He doesn't want them all to act like servants forever. It's annoying him. There has to be a hierarchy for missions and security issues, but Luke values freedom highly, and his men matter to him."

"Yeah, I know. The rest of us came here looking for a different life. The dragons came here to become servants so they could be what they are. Blaze is getting better. He loosened up a bit. I got him to talk with me as a man last night. He started calling me 'Fangs' instead of 'my king'."

"One dragon at a time. Fangs, staves competitions may help us unify the pack. I hope we have enough time to solidify before we have a serious confrontation."

Fox's countenance grew serious as his smile faded.

"I thought you ought to know. I may have a lead on Rake. The bears who helped me rescue Isabell in California and sent Melody to us, are good men. They heard what happened, and they offered to help hunt the bastard. I got a tip. He was on the west coast. Jace and Scar are checking it out for us."

"Damn, I hope they find the scum. He deserves whatever Luke decides and then some."

Andrei told Fox the truth. Some people didn't deserve to be classified as people. Rake was one of them.

"I agree. Nadine down for the count?"

"Yeah, you down to get some work done?"

"Sure thing. I'll join you in a few. Let me take care of the stuff in the sink."

Andrei smiled and headed out to the garage. Fox loved to play with the food. Whatever was in the sink would be on the table at twilight dinner. Andrei didn't eat, but he kept the peace for his friends who did. No one referenced Fox's guilty pleasure.

The one thing Andrei was certain of? He would lose at staves later. He and Blaze would have another chance to spar on a future date.

Andrei had to make it last long enough to make it a good show, then make a slight mistake. There was no way Andrei could make the dragon look bad in front of his sorceress.

CHAPTER NINE

As Badly As

B^{*laze*}

The day went well. He had breakfast with Jewel, and they worked on her business model. How lucky could a dragon get? Jewel worked with treasure.

She sold treasure to gain more treasure. The dragon in him was into her business model as much as she was. If she wasn't to be a Valkyrie, he wasn't a dragon. The morning flew by, and they stopped work to grab lunch.

Lightning and Cloud were in the dining room having lunch as well. Ember and Flower arrived a few minutes later. Jewel and Flower got involved in sharing the worst customer stories with Cloud.

All three women had owned their businesses before they got caught up in Elliot's macabre experiment. Blaze and his brothers did what guys always did. They focused on the upcoming sparring competition.

"So, are you planning on letting the vampire win?" Ember asked.

Blaze quirked his brow at his brother.

"No. But it is a quandary. I know well that he is Ruiri, but it feels different here. I respect Fangs. The man has some skills, and he's fast. I hope for a good match."

"Flame thinks we should make it look good, but let the Ruiri win," Ember noted.

After the way the Ruiri in the past had treated Flame, it made sense for Flame to think that way. Ember rarely disagreed with Flame's assessment for similar reasons.

"Jewel pointed out to me yesterday how different it is here than what we dealt with in Leinster. Fangs deserves a fair competition. It's not as if I can wait for my king to die and hope for a better replacement. The Ruiri here are all immortals. I have thought about it. If I can, I would prefer to work with mutual respect. Smoke managed it. It can be done."

Ember and Lightning both nodded in agreeable comprehension.

Blaze heard his brothers' concern and knew they wanted to know his mind because Blaze would have to be the one to approach Flame.

Flame had been the last of them to agree to be collared again. He'd always been the life of the party, a charismatic individual. He'd enjoyed a unique status under his first Ruiri, paraded about in grand style.

Flame of all the dragons had at first enjoyed the new life he had. He had been a debonair lady's man in real life, and he became so again even as a dragon. What the next Ruiri had done to Flame was so grievously wrong. Even Blaze cringed when he thought about it, and he had tortured men as his job for long years as the Ri ruirech's dungeon master.

It had been too late for Blaze to stop any of it when it happened, and it left Flame in a terrible state for a long time.

He and Blaze had become much closer to one another afterward. Blaze had been the one to convince Flame to serve again.

"I'll speak to him. He'll hear my words. He has Nightshade. Don't fear. She'll stay and work with

Mihaela and Angel. Luke wants to hire her to be a dance and fitness instructor for the Athletic Center. I've seen Flame with her. Nightshade is his redemption. Even if he doesn't know it. He won't leave her."

"Is it true she can't hunt?" Ember asked.

"Flame's been working with her, but whoever turned her vjestice taught her nothing. He hasn't bothered to teach her how to control the servants yet and has even asked the other vampires to allow him the honor of teaching her. She's skittish and lacks the focus to control the allure. At best, it only works partially. It feels as if she's wearing delicate perfume instead of drawing you in as it should."

The women drew to the conversation and listened to Blaze.

"Who turned her into a vjestice? Did she say?" Lightning asked.

"She claimed three men turned her."

Flower answered as Ember put his arm around her.

"She said they had pointed teeth. She has three-bite wound scars."

"Dragons turned her with magic then. No wonder her eyes are black. They likely took turns feeding her the dragon blood. She would have needed to survive the turning," Lightning surmised.

"They took turns trying to make a thrall rider who could serve them all, but they wound up with a damaged vjestice."

Flower trembled. Ember let the dragon fire dance over her where they touched. She smiled at him with her thanks.

"Valkyries have to choose it. Ash was right. Inferno, Pyro, and Blast are wrong. Everything about those three dragons seemed evil."

Ember surmised which dragons had tortured Nightshade.

"It took Flame two days to convince Nightshade he wasn't like them and she could trust him." Blaze said.

"I think he's feeding her, too. There is no blood in the fridge, and she can't hunt. He turned his riders in the past," Lightning said.

Blaze nodded. It made sense. Flame was desperate to win her. He probably allowed her to drink from him because his magic would sustain her more easily.

Blaze hoped his brother was smart about it. It was a forbidden act for a dragon to bleed for another except to save a life or feed the Valkyrie. Dragon blood was addictive and caused women to become thralls.

"Don't tell Ash," Blaze admonished them.

They all nodded. None of them wanted to interfere after what had happened in the past with Flame's riders. Flame knew more about vampires than likely any other dragon alive.

If Ash thought Flame might accidentally turn Hannah into a thrall, if he learned Flame fed her from his vein, he would separate the two of them. None of them were better equipped to deal with a vjestice vampire than the one dragon among them who had turned his riders into vjestice vampires. Nightshade needed Flame as badly as Flame needed Nightshade.

CHAPTER TEN

Jewel Groaned

Blaze

When lunch ended, Blaze and Jewel went back to the room, and Blaze picked up his laptop, thinking of picking up where they had left off.

Jewel mumbled something under her breath. The next minute, he stood in the middle of the room, minus all of his clothes. He turned to look at Jewel. She had her hand over her mouth, but her eyes remained glued to his.

"What's going on?"

"I took off my shoes, but somehow..."

She stopped speaking as he faced her.

Jewel stared at him. Blaze thought her appreciation might be a good thing. They should go slow, but if she liked how he looked, he wasn't about to make her stop. After a minute, he lifted his arms and spun slowly around so she could see him in his entirety.

Jewel giggled at his antics.

"I'm sorry. My magic is still a bit off."

"I'm glad it happened here instead of in the living room. Where did my clothes go?"

"I intended to send my shoes to the closet."

Blaze walked over to the closet and found his clothes in a shoebox at the bottom of the closet. How did taking off one's shoes turn into a naked dragon?

"Are you sure that's all you were thinking about?"

Blaze grinned as he picked his clothes out of the shoe box.

Jewel blushed prettily.

"I had been thinking before about how sexy you looked."

She didn't meet his eyes as she spoke. Embarrassed, she didn't want to lie because it wouldn't help untangle the issue.

"So taking off your shoes got mixed with wondering what I looked like naked, and I wound up naked. It seems to me, my being naked was more important to you than getting your shoes put away."

She smiled at him, and she walked over to him. Jewel did the most ridiculous thing. She traced her finger over his dragon tattoo.

It was nothing really, but she was his mate. She wanted to touch him. He held his breath, afraid to breathe and ruin the moment.

He soaked in the feel of her fingers on his skin. Heat traveled through his body, radiating from the point on his chest where her fingers made contact.

"I like this. It's nice."

Jewel spoke with the same breathlessness she had when he kissed her.

Blaze wasn't sure if she meant to compliment his tattoo or the chemistry between them when they touched. He needed to stop her, but it was hard when she had been the one who started it.

"I had it done not long after the iron collar broke when I feared I would never shift again. I wanted a reminder of what I am."

He whispered the words as breathless as she was.

"Will you kiss me again?"

He grabbed her before she could change her mind.

His lips descended on hers, and he kissed her. He had wanted to kiss her again since she had goaded him into it the first time. She should be his.

He couldn't lose control and forget himself in the kiss. He couldn't deny his mate's request for him, either.

Blaze had long ago mastered the sexual arts, but with her, it mattered. It felt as if his entire being was on fire. No woman had ever made him burn for her before.

He held her body close to his as his lips played over hers. He demanded entrance into her mouth with his tongue, and she granted it immediately. She was light to his dark, and nothing had ever felt so perfect.

The dragon fire swirled over them as he deepened the kiss and tasted her mouth. The white light of her magic swirled with the flames and made his soul burn.

Blaze wanted her, and she kissed him back. He finally broke the kiss so he could breathe as he kissed down the side of her neck. Jewel moaned.

"Blaze, I need you to prove it to me. I have to know if I'm your mate. I don't want this if it won't go anywhere."

Her words were a barely breathed response. Blaze groaned. Was she even ready to deal with it when he proved it to her? He knew how to do it without sex, but he was too far gone. He needed to love her properly. Blaze didn't want her to have regrets.

"I want to love you? Will you accept me as your dragon lover?"

Blaze sucked her earlobe into his mouth.

He manipulated her answer, but he was determined to make it feel good for her. Grace didn't understand, but she would never have another after him. Just the first kiss had been past the point of no return.

Grace caught her breath, then she did the one thing she shouldn't have. She begged him. All thoughts of keeping things under control disappeared when she did that.

He stripped her out of her blouse and skirt faster than she'd probably ever been able to undress. She lay naked on the bed, suffering his kisses and moaning in his ear as her hands roamed over his back.

He was so lost to her. She was soft, and he needed to feel her. Listening to the way she breathed and moaned drove the madness of his desire for her.

Blaze knelt between her thighs and positioned himself to enter her. It had to be slow. He knew he couldn't hurry it or hurt her. He would love her thoroughly.

"We'll go slow. I won't hurt you. I want you to feel me loving you, and you'll know it. Look at me. Don't look away. Get lost in my eyes and try to see into me. When you shatter, keep looking at me. I will have you."

Blaze held her gaze for a moment longer as she relaxed. When he began moving into her, she caught her breath. He went slowly as he promised.

Blaze needed to fill her. If he could, he would imprint himself on her so she could know him without fear. His hands caressed her as he entered her, gliding over her arms and her breasts.

When her eyes grew wide, he whispered to her.

"You are with me, Jewel. Stay with me. Let me love you as you need me to. Let me prove to you what you are for me."

She kept her eyes on him and stayed calm under his hands. She trusted him, which gave him a rush of pleasure.

His voice eased her anxiety and, looking at him, helped her associate him with everything she felt. Blaze filled her and touched her center. Jewel groaned.

CHAPTER ELEVEN

Out Of The Question

Blaze

"Please Blaze. You're too much."

She wasn't in any pain. Grace wasn't used to being stretched so completely by her lover. He stilled inside her and held himself there, waiting for her to move. When she moved, he moved.

When he stroked her, she moaned long and low. He never wanted to stop. Her eyes slipped almost closed in pleasure.

"Don't close your eyes, Jewel. Look at me. I need you to see me. Your dragon is loving you. You must stay with me. Know you belong to me."

His voice was low and throaty.

Speaking to her became difficult. She felt too good as he eased in and out of her. Time had stopped for them. He loved her, and she slipped into the rhythm of his love.

He felt her body tighten around him as he leaned into her. She was so close to falling over the edge. He didn't speed up. He continued and let her climax build slowly.

He would follow her over the precipice when she fell apart. One more stroke, and she lost herself.

Blaze held her head as her body writhed beneath him, clenching him over and over. She screamed his name out as she came hard. It pushed him over the edge after her, and he spilled himself deep inside her, groaning her name. He didn't allow her to look away.

She cried out in surprise when the link built like a purple candle flame in her mind. He smiled at her as his cock slowly withdrew from her.

Blaze could feel her curiosity in the link. Her mind touched the link, and his love and desire for his mate tumbled into her mind, filling and stretching it tight as his cock stretched her body.

Awe and raw desire flooded back at him. It excited Jewel when the link had worked. He could feel her mind register her body's soreness from their lovemaking, but it felt good for her. She smiled, even though her eyes had finally slipped closed.

The white candle flame in his mind dumped her feelings into his head. Blaze wanted to drown in her emotions. They were pure.

Blaze had proven to her she was his mate. He had given her the knowledge she could have him, keep him, love him. It wouldn't be a onetime thing.

She was to be his Valkyrie. They had time, but he'd linked with his mate. He wouldn't let her go now.

Jewel was his treasure. Blaze was fiercely protective of her. Linking with her wasn't the same as bonding with her.

He'd given her his blood. The magic pressed him to bond with her.

She wasn't ready for it. He tightened his control over himself. She needed time to become accustomed to him as her lover.

Blaze promised to go slow with her. Jewel needed slow and steady. She wasn't a shifter. Jewel needed her proof. He had to keep her safe, but he had to warn her about the magic. She needed to know.

"Can you feel it, Jewel? Do you understand now what I meant when I said you were everything?"

She opened her eyes and looked up, smiling at him.

"This is what you felt all along? You're a rock of patience, Blaze. How did you wait?"

Blaze laughed.

"You weren't ready. Pushing the only woman I ever truly desired away from me was never an option for me."

"Thank you for proving it to me. I wanted you to be real. You were too sexy, and you are a dark magic. They warned me to stay away from what you are. Sorceresses fear the dark arts. I was afraid you had found me and saw your chance to gain control of my magic."

She shied away from him a bit, then she added the statement he'd already committed to.

"Can we still go slow?"

"I promise. I'll keep it slow. Grace, I have to warn you. You changed the game. I gave you my blood to save you. The magic pushes me to bond with you, to finish the ritual. I need you to be careful because I spent three centuries never being allowed to say 'no'. I'm a dragon, forced to serve. If you ask me, it will be twice as hard for me. My nature never wishes to deny you anything. Do you understand?"

She nodded.

She wasn't ready to make any demands of him.

"Never run from me. The dragon in me will give chase. You're a treasure to me. I can't allow another an opportunity to steal you from me. If you tried to fade, I would go into the Netherworld to bring you back. I have the patience to wait for you, but only so long as I believe I'll have you as mine."

Blaze needed to be clear to her. She wasn't a shifter. He couldn't assume she would know.

"Blaze, when you went into the warehouse, you already knew I was there, didn't you?"

"You were why I agreed with my brothers to come here. Luke knew where you were. Fox had scouted the warehouses earlier in the week. Luke waited for us to man the mission, and he struck on a Friday night because the area would be a ghost town. We knew you were all there."

Blaze didn't lie to her. The truth would only continue to enforce her trust in him.

"I want this with you."

Blaze kissed her.

There was nothing in the dream he wanted more than her. Jewel snuggled against him. He stroked her hair and held her. She needed his strength, and he gave it to her. Holding her close felt too good.

They lay in one another's arms for a long time, drowsing and petting one another as a form of after play. He refused to allow things to go anywhere further, as hurting her was out of the question.

CHAPTER TWELVE

Throw The Match

B^{*laze*}

Twilight dinner was excellent. The excitement ran deep. Everyone in residence at Draoithe was in high spirits. The competition schedule hung on the refrigerator at Fox's house. The dragons listened as Fox and Andrei retold their sparring session.

As dinner wound down, Blaze caught Flame's attention. They needed to talk. Things needed to be different with the Dire Wolf King. They met on the deck. Jewel and Nightshade were with them.

"Flame, I wanted to talk to you. Can we walk? It's not for everyone to hear."

Flame looked at Nightshade, and Blaze nodded. He wouldn't leave Jewel behind, either. They walked away from the group. As they neared the treeline of the green belt, Flame started the conversation.

"What's up, bro?"

"Lightning and Ember are worried you won't take a win against a Ruiri because you fear retribution."

Blaze didn't hold back.

"Did you draw the short straw on hitting me up about it?"

Flame laughed coldly.

"No. I felt the same way until last night. I didn't believe Luke when he said he didn't want the titles and all the etiquette, but I've watched the people here. Luke uses the pack to create order in Draoithe's society. The men he chooses as Ruiri are all diverse, but none of them are 'yes' men. He has chosen men he respects. He even has the Ri bannach as council members."

"What are you saying?"

Flame looked suspicious, but Blaze had no reason to con his old friend.

"This time it's different. There are no petty human kings. The Dire Wolf King is an actual direwolf. Give Luke a chance. Give this place a chance. Kallik gave you one. Andrei has done the same for me.

Smoke had a relationship with Fox based on mutual respect before, and they still have it. These men are kings like he was. Like he still is."

"I don't know."

Flame shook his head.

"I'm trying. I want it to be different as much as you do. Everything we believed about this venture has proven to be true so far. I see what you see. It won't come easy for me, but Mihaela and Nightshade spent Monday evening trying to discover why her allure doesn't work. Kallik even asked me if I would discuss vampires with him. He offered me some good advice and a new perspective."

Flame shook his head again.

He paused, trying to find the right words to explain. Blaze was happy to hear Flame sought help for Nightshade. It meant his obsession hadn't descended into madness.

"Kallik asked. He didn't simply decide and do it. Kallik approached me as an equal. He didn't wish to approach Nightshade because he didn't want me to interpret it wrong. He acted as if it mattered to him if he respected my claim to Nightshade."

Blaze nodded. Fangs had been as respectful to him the night before.

"Flame, are you feeding her?"

Flame punched him. Was he Smoke to never see it coming when Ember clocked him?

He hadn't seen it coming. Blaze slipped to one knee before he tackled Flame to the ground.

What the fuck were they doing? He just asked a question!

Why would Flame attack him? Something was seriously wrong with Flame.

They wrestled with one another for several minutes, each getting several punches in on the other. When they got back to their feet, Blaze pushed Flame away from him, still confused about why they were even fighting.

"I won't let you take her from me. No one will take her."

Flame hissed at him. Dragon fire spread over his clenched fists.

Blaze didn't want to take Nightshade from Flame. Where had his brother gotten that idea?

"I don't want to take her from you. I wanted to know if there was a way I could help you."

Blaze hissed back, still panting.

He knew he had a black eye, and blood dripped into his right eye from a cut above it. Flame sported a busted lip, and the left side of his jaw was turning purple.

Dragons were invincible in that death didn't last, but fights still hurt, and death still happened.

Flame looked at Nightshade and Jewel, who had backed away from the scene. Confused but still agitated, the scene finally clicked for Blaze in an instant.

"You linked with her, didn't you?"

Blaze grinned at his brother.

Blaze knew where the problem was. He looked at Nightshade. Her eyes were green, not black. Flame figured out how to fix his mate, and he wasn't about to allow anything to get in the way, not even his best friend.

Blaze knew who Flame was. His friend was a good man. He'd always been the best of them.

Flame stood still for a minute as the realization of what they had done washed over him. Blaze knew his brother meant to keep the woman he saw as his treasure from being separated from him.

The murder of his vjestice riders devastated Flame. He would go to any lengths necessary to protect and keep Nightshade.

Even if Flame never saw it. Nightshade was his redemption.

Flame slowly grinned at Blaze and nodded his head. Blaze had been the brother who helped Flame put his life back together centuries ago.

Blaze nodded at Jewel. He let her feel his relief. A smile ghosted over her face. Both of the women went to their dragons.

"Sorry, Blaze. I lost it. I won't give her up."

Flame hung his head for a minute. The magic had pushed him over the edge.

"We're good, Flame. No worries. I'd rather have a shiner from you than lose my brother. I only asked because I know Ash. Look, none of us has the expertise you do. Are you okay? Do you need anything?"

"No. It's cool. Yeah, I've been feeding her every morning at dawn. I have it under control. I won't have her become a thrall. The deer's blood didn't stop the thirst. Mine did."

Nightshade blushed, embarrassed, and looked away.

Blaze extended his hand to his brother.

"If you need help, Flame?"

Flame grasped Blaze's forearm.

"You will be the first to know."

Flame nodded.

"I have been thinking about what you said. I need it to be different this time, same as we all do."

They walked back, so Blaze could get ready for the competition. Blaze would compete honestly.

He never thought for a minute Andrei might throw the match.

CHAPTER THIRTEEN
Headed For

Andrei

When Blaze stepped onto the deck behind Fox's house, Andrei raised his brow at his opponent's appearance. It might be late, but most immortals had excellent vision, even with no lights.

"Blaze, are you up for this?"

"I'm good. Minor miscommunication. It's settled."

Blaze grinned at him. Andrei nodded.

Blaze

Blaze had fought many times, looking and feeling far worse than he did at that moment. He was a dragon.

In a few hours, no evidence would remain. The cut above his eye was almost healed. There was a plus upside to being a dragon shifter with a rider. After his encounter with Jewel earlier, he would simply regenerate at dawn and erase any damage.

The entire population of Draoithe had turned out to see the duel. Blaze marked Jewel's location. She stood next to Nadine.

It was odd to him she'd chosen to ally herself with the vjestice eagle, but he could feel she wasn't comfortable with the other men. He wasn't unhappy with her decision.

Andrei

Andrei had marked Nadine's place as well. Her choice pleased him, even though he wasn't a shifter. The two women talked shop. They both wielded magic, which could cast spells.

Andrei and Blaze crossed staves and led off on the left foot. The slow click-clack of the wood striking wood was the only sound once they began. Everyone watched.

There were no rules about not speaking. The audience remained hyper-focused on the duel to continue with their conversations.

The two combatants felt each other out, tracking style, and noting weaknesses in their opponent. The duel picked up speed, and the staves flew fast through the air as the two men danced around one another.

There was no magic being used, but both men were long-practiced fighters. Andrei had never used his magic in any staff competition before. It would've cost him his life at the enclave. Modern vampire society forbade the existence of an unbound zduhaci.

Blaze

Dragons learned to use the staff and spear without their magic as well. Fire and wood didn't work well together in combat unless the aim was to get warm.

Dragon fire couldn't harm a dragon, so it was rare they had a use for it in a duel. They sparred mostly with one another and, in rare cases, the knights.

Who wished to incinerate a worthy sparring partner? It rather defeated the purpose.

Andrei was fast. Blaze had a height and reach advantage. Both men's skill level was high.

Blaze had thought of winning handily over the slender shorter vampire, but he found himself pressed many times. Blaze had spent many more years training with the weapon, but it didn't seem to be a real advantage.

Blaze outweighed the vampire by nearly a hundred pounds and was more than half a foot taller, but Andrei used it to his advantage. He maneuvered the staff in and out around the dragon faster than Blaze could always effectively counter.

Blaze knew immediately he would want serious practice in the future. About fifteen minutes into the duel, he knew Andrei had outmatched him.

They continued the parry and thrust of the staves for another five minutes. Each man sported several visible bruises on the arms. Andrei had a red welt on his right side. Blaze had several circular bruises on his thighs from the thrust of the staff.

Andrei

Andrei had expected Blaze to be good, but the man nearly outmatched him. He had intended to lose by throwing the match, but he was afraid he might lose for real.

It wouldn't be the pretty show he had imagined. The dragon threw the staff from one hand to the other, but never let it go.

At some point, Andrei realized he had the dragon. Blaze was good, but he lacked the stamina for a protracted duel. Andrei knew it was only a matter of time. He had to let the dragon win.

Andrei swept Blaze's feet out from under him, but Blaze launched the staff into the air, landed on his hands, and kicked upwards hard. Andrei's staff went flying. Blaze allowed the kick to flip him over.

He landed on his feet and held out his hand for his staff to smack his palm as gravity brought it back down from the sky.

Andrei made eye contact with Flame. The man had been watching the bout intensely, as if he were the one Andrei fought. Andrei winked at Flame.

Blaze

Blaze advanced against Andrei. In moments, Blaze had him penned and Andrei's staff was in Blaze's hand.

"Do you yield?"

Andrei spread his hands in defeat.

"I yield."

Andrei spoke with a bit of surprise.

Forty minutes had passed. Both men breathed hard as their friends clapped and cheered. It had been an excellent match. Blaze smiled at his king. Maybe things could be different.

Andrei

Andrei extended his hand to the first opponent to beat him in over fifty years. He grinned at Blaze. Blaze clasped Andrei's right forearm and grinned back at the vampire.

"I swear, I honestly thought you had me for a minute, Fangs."

"Put me down for the rematch. First, teach me the handstand move. That, I wasn't expecting."

Blaze nodded. Andrei may have lost the match, but he'd won a dragon as a friend. That was far more important to him than chalking up another staves victory.

When the two men broke apart, Blaze embraced an enthusiastic Jewel. Andrei had made the right decision to throw the match. After a few pats on the back, the audience dispersed and left Blaze holding his Jewel. Andrei fell into his eagle and headed for a shower.

CHAPTER FOURTEEN

Begging For Him

Blaze

"That was awesome! You were fantastic."

"You're going to get all sweaty, Jewel."

Blaze teased her as he held her close.

"Then I'll smell like juniper and whiskey."

Blaze could feel how excited she had been. Winning the duel had made him seem bigger to her. He hadn't considered how winning or losing the duel would have made him look in her eyes.

The random thought Fangs had deliberately lost crossed his mind. Would Andrei deliberately throw the match just to make Blaze look better?

Had he been so serious about claiming friendship? He would have to find out later.

"Come with me to get a shower?"

She nodded, and he scooped her up and swung her around in his arms as he walked back to the house. The dew wetted his feet, and he had a lot of bruises for the day, but Jewel was happy. There was no fear in the link between them. She giggled in his arms as he kissed her.

He set her back on her feet on the porch, and they walked in the back door into the kitchen hand-in-hand.

Smoke and Char congratulated him on his win again and turned back to their work on the laptops. Ice and Angel waved at them as they made their way down the hall to the bathroom.

The minute the door closed behind them, Blaze backed her up against the wall and caged her there with his arms as he bent his head to kiss her again.

Her hands pressed against his chest. He could feel her desire for him in the link and saying 'no' was not an option, not for either of them.

The adrenaline from the duel with Fangs hadn't worn off yet. He knew he had to be easy with her, but he would take her.

She stripped off her clothes when he broke the kiss. Her lips were puffy. Blaze had kissed her too hard.

She didn't back away from him. Instead, she prepared to join him in the shower.

Blaze dropped his joggers and his boxers to the floor. He turned the water on cold. It would all turn to steam, anyway.

The dragon fire ignited as he stepped into the shower with her. The steam filled the room. It was like making love in a warm fog.

She was so sexy, and he needed her so badly. He could feel her excitement rise. He soaped her, and she soaped him. Their hands roamed over the other's body.

Jewel turned beneath the water and wet her hair as she rinsed off the lather, then she shifted quickly away from the cold water. She turned her back to him to get the shampoo, and he was lost.

He was inside her deep, as he pressed her up against the shower wall. Blaze groaned at the feel of her slick, wet heat.

He could feel her fear. She had frozen. He tangled his right hand into her wet hair and pulled her head back against his chest, so her body arched for him to press into her further.

"Give me your fear. Command your dragon, Jewel."

He whispered the words hoarsely in her ear. His cock twitched inside her. She moaned, but she was still afraid.

"Order me to stop. Tell me you don't want me to love you."

He urged her to speak of her fear.

His left hand caressed and squeezed her left breast. She panted, her desire warred with her fear.

"Tell me, *no*," he breathed against her ear as his hand slipped down the plane of her stomach.

His fingers swirled over her navel and followed a line down to her mound.

"I need you, Jewel. I'm going to take you as a dragon rider. Let go of the fear. Feel my strength. Take it."

She gasped.

His fingers found her nub and danced upon it as he withdrew his cock from her. She sucked in a breath.

He slammed back into her hard. She cried out in pleasure. His fingers stroked over her clit as his cock rubbed her pussy walls raw with friction.

Blaze took her hard and fast from behind. He pressed into her center over and over. He felt her initial fear dissipate in the steam surrounding them.

Jewel spiraled to the pinnacle of pleasure, and Blaze wanted her to shatter hard. He didn't, couldn't stop. He wanted to erase her fear.

He needed her to want to explore the adventure with him. He felt his balls draw up as she cried out in ecstasy. She came hard on him, tightening on his shaft, increasing his pleasure, and he finished himself deep inside her.

Jewel trembled in his arms as he withdrew from her. He'd exhausted her. But he slowly erased her fear.

Blaze had to build her trust in him. He needed her to seek her pleasure with him, to need him to love her.

Blaze turned the warmer water on and let his flames extinguish. He lathered her platinum blonde hair as he held her to him, then he turned her and rinsed her hair. He washed his hair quickly with one hand as he held her next to him.

He carried her out of the shower. She wasn't in pain. She'd traded him her fear, and now she needed his strength.

He set her easily on the vanity. He wrapped her in a towel, then he wrapped one around his waist and carried her out of the bathroom, just as he had the first time he'd bathed her.

Once inside the room they shared, he kicked the door closed. He discarded their towels and lay down with her gently. Her hands had been around his neck, but they slid down to his chest as she sighed into his embrace.

Blaze pulled the covers over her and let her drift away to sleep. He watched her sleep for a long time.

The magic pressed him hard to claim her, but he had to wait for her to choose it. If it were up to him, he would have her begging for him to bite her.

CHAPTER FIFTEEN

Join The Pack

Grace

Friday passed in a haze. Blaze loved her every time her desire for him rose and touched his mind on the link. He apologized to her once. He was afraid it was too much, but to him, it felt as if she asked him for it.

He was talented. She felt inept, but he continued to return to her. He told her how beautiful she was to him, and how sexy he found her to be.

Blaze was charming and thoughtful. He never loved her the same way twice. He left her exhausted again Friday evening. Grace just curled up into him and slept soundly in his arms until morning.

It wasn't until later she knew he'd left to help his brother at four in the morning. Flame had broken some laws dragons couldn't break. That was unsurprising.

"I'm confused Blaze. Why are you angry with Ash?"

Grace asked as they dressed for the day.

Blaze blew out his breath.

"I shouldn't be. Flame called the magic. He wanted absolution, but he should have received it five hundred years ago. If he had, what happened today wouldn't have been necessary. Flame carried guilt for far too long because Ash believed a lie and denied Flame a genuine chance to explain. Flame was so broken-hearted and grief-stricken over what happened to the vjestice riders he allowed Ash to get away with relieving him of his responsibilities. Ash preferred to resolve the issue and placate the Ruiri when he should have absolved Flame."

"You can't fault Ash for doing what he thought was best."

Blaze had a dark side, and he wanted things to be black and white when they were usually grey.

"No, but I can fault the Lord of Dragons for taking the easy way out. Flame was the best of us, and what Ash did was effectively make him the least of us."

"Blaze, did Ash ask to be made what he is?"

Blaze turned on her and stared at her. He stood frozen. She could practically realize the shine on her dark dragon. He knew the truth then.

Ash had the responsibility of being the dragons' diplomat. He had the hardest task, and he constantly juggled all their needs and issues, as well as his own.

He wasn't perfect, and he'd asked for none of it. Not then or now. Even Grace could see Blaze had gotten hurt by the fallout.

Blaze pulled her to him and kissed her deeply.

"Thank you, Jewel. I needed to be reminded Ash is my brother, too."

Saturday morning after breakfast, they finally got some work done. She'd been too sore to contemplate any more sexual activity. By lunch, she talked excitedly with several of the dragons and women at the house about the ceremonies and the *Run*. She had a lot of questions.

That evening she would go with Blaze to Draoithe to see the pack submission ceremony for Griz and Melody and watch Kallik, Mihaela, Ryker, and Lily take their oaths to become Ruiri and Ri bannach and join the Druid Pack Council.

Grace wasn't a shifter, so the pack mentality didn't come easy to her. After lunch, Blaze tried to explain how it worked.

"Okay, but why do I join the pack? I'm not a shifter."

"You don't have to be a shifter to submit to the alphas in a pack. You're agreeing to follow Luke and Eli as the leaders of the society. In a pack, every member is equal. They all contribute to the welfare of the group. If an issue arises which needs to be resolved, Luke and Eli decide."

"I don't understand. I thought Luke decided."

"Luke leads the pack, but not without Eli. Eli is a tiger. Tigers are more solitary animals. Eli relies on Luke's judgment, but if she gives an order, even he won't argue with her. No pack operates without both an alpha male and an alpha female. There must be a balance of power."

"So why the titles and the hierarchy of Ruiri and Ri bannach?"

"Druid fealty oaths guarantee loyalty. Luke is avoiding infiltration of the pack by an outsider. He also doesn't like to lead alone. He wants a council of advisors to help him make the best decisions for Draoithe. Hell, he doesn't even own it alone. Fox and Javier are both equal partners with him in the business."

"Then how do dragons and Valkyrie fit in?"

Grace thought she understood the rest, but the dragons seemed to be a wild card.

"When Luke became the Ri ruirech by the Ruiri, he hoped to use the druid magic as a defensive measure. One more layer of protection, if you will. Fox was unaware that dragons also had a connection to the druid magic. He thought we were gone from the dream because we slept with no king to serve. When Fox swore fealty, the dragons were called to serve. Fox was born touching the magic which created dragons. My brothers and I had originally all served the same king Fox served in his youth. One dragon knight serves each king as a war counselor."

Blaze tried to explain, but Grace didn't understand the medieval social hierarchy. She shook her head.

"Think of each king as a castle filled with all the people who would have lived in a castle, peasants, knights, the king's family, visitors, servants, skilled craft workers, etc. The king handles all of it. Each king had a dragon as his lead knight. Dragons are the protectors of the realm. We enforced his law, policed his subjects, and protected his interests."

"But Luke, Fox, and Fangs don't have castles."

"No, but they have the power to rule one. They each have a stake in Draoithe. Just as the old Ruiri of Leinster had a castle and grounds, Fangs and Kallik each controlled one-fourteenth of Draoithe as their part of joining the council. So the dragons will protect the kings' interests, even if it isn't technically a stone castle. There are servants here already. As the pack grows, people will take up work with the Ruiri and the Ri bannach. Dragons will protect them as subjects of the Ruiri."

"Dragons are invincible, so if a fight had to be broken up, who better to deal with it?"

Grace understood.

"This is my purpose for existence. If the kings needed to fight to protect their land, dragons are serious weapons on the battlefield. Luke sees us as mission assets. My brothers and I are a well-coordinated fighting team."

"What about you? Will you join the pack?"

CHAPTER SIXTEEN
A Little Hesitant

Grace

None of the dragons were pack members. Why not?

"Without a Valkyrie, Luke won't accept any of us. His honor won't tolerate the obvious disrespect to women in the rider system dragons once used. The mental suffering the dragons suffered would torment him as well. His people matter to him. Dragons are also simply too dangerous. He needs us to be free to protect the pack. He seeks the balance."

Blaze seemed distant. He needed his Valkyrie to join the pack. He'd repeatedly never pressed her. If they never mated, he could never join the pack, but he would never ask it of her.

"Grace, I need to meet with Flame at four in the garage. I need to practice. It may seem strange to you, but I'm still a dragon. I have a military position. Not training this past week wasn't good. Andrei was right about the staff being a good way to clear the mind. Flame owes me a left-handed lesson after the stunt he pulled this morning. Hannah has made him so much more of the brother I learned to be a dragon with. I must be what I am, and I need to speak with Ash. Will you be alright?"

"Yes, I'll be fine. I need to think some things through. Go ahead."

She smiled at him. Blaze had been eagerly anticipating the Thursday night staves. Men were silly about their competitions.

His friendship with his brother was deep. She liked that side of him. He kissed her and left her sitting in the living room. She could hear Smoke and Angel talking quietly in the dining room, but she needed to sit still and think.

Blaze came back a few minutes later to call her to see a show, interrupting her thoughts.

"Do you guys want to see a show? Flame taught Nightshade how to use her allure. She has Ash, and she's still pissed off because he ruined the end of her night out with Flame. She wants to see Flame kick Ash's ass."

Smoke, Angel, and Jewel all followed him into the garage.

Grace watched, and it was fun knowing Nightshade had set it all up and Flame wasn't upset. Maybe Ash would unwind a bit.

Grace laughed with Smoke and Angel as they left the garage. Blaze had been right. It was a show worth watching. Nightshade got her revenge. Flame was an excellent champion for her.

It was good to see Hannah happier. If she was good for Flame, he was as good for her. Blaze had explained how Flame had died to be with her. They were good together.

When the show was over and everyone had laughed, she left Smoke and Angel and went back to tracking her thoughts about Blaze. Grace had felt his desire to join the pack. If he joined, the Druid pack would treat him as an equal. No longer would the Druid pack view him as a dragon, as less than a person, merely a servant. He would be free, but she knew he didn't want her because of it.

Blaze was serious-minded and stoic, a silent, introspective man. Grace felt his desire for the type of friendship Fox and Smoke shared with his Ruiri,

Andrei. He was far more relaxed with the dragons than with the other people at Draoithe.

Would he be so silent if he weren't always bowing and scraping at someone else? He wasn't that way with Flame. They had an old, deep friendship.

Flame seemed to want the same thing as Blaze. Blaze had suffered with Flame. Both men wanted things to be different at Draoithe than they had been in the past.

Blaze hoped. He liked Andrei. He'd even taken the chance to spar with the vampire and won.

Blaze had been afraid to take the step. As a serving dragon, people had never treated Blaze as a person. He'd always been a tool. All the dragons had suffered the same injustices.

Blaze had said he came to serve Luke and by default be Andrei's dragon. Blaze had also come for her. He needed her as his mate, but he also needed her to be his Valkyrie so he could be free, seen as an equal, and treated as a person. She could finish his dream as no other person could.

He could only really be fully the dragon he was if he had his Valkyrie. Blaze wanted his mate as his Valkyrie. He wanted Grace. He'd waited six centuries for her.

The longer Grace knew Blaze, the more she fell for him. He was beyond amazing as a lover, and he'd been nothing but her kind man. Blaze was all male and pure alpha, but she was safe with him. He'd traded his strength for her fear.

Would he be willing to trade again when she bonded with him? She was afraid. He had a dark side. She'd seen it the day she'd accidentally walked into her servant.

He'd been like a knight in shining armor, though. He even took his training seriously. Watching him coordinate his life so he remained who he was while he made a place for her in it so he could protect her and share his life with her made him more endearing.

Lost in her thoughts when he spoke to her, she startled. How long had he been watching her?

"Jewel, I think you should take up staff practice to help you clear your thoughts. It works. I wanted to know if you will come with me? I want to share something you need to see."

Blaze asked as he studied her feelings while she thought. She nodded, and they walked out of the house in the late afternoon summer sun. They crossed the little bridge into the trees of the greenbelt.

"I want to show you the other side of me and share my dragon with you. I want you to know all about me. Will you be my rider and accept my oath? Will you fly with a dragon?"

Excited, Grace nodded and followed him into the woods behind the creek. Grace was afraid, but she wanted to try.

"What do I have to do?"

She asked, and just like that, he took her fear and gave her his strength.

Blaze explained. She accepted his oath, and he stripped off his clothes. She might never tire of seeing him naked. He was sexy. Then she watched the flame trace over him until a magnificent dragon stood before her.

Blaze was a grey which started light on his head but faded to a dark grey on his feet with silver-grey claws and horns with blue-black tail spikes and wing bones. His hair was blue black with streaks of silver grey. He was as tall as a large draft horse, and the blue-black leather wings made him seem even larger. She could feel the magic swirling around him.

She understood why he wanted to be a dragon. He was more dominant in his dragon form. She agreed to fly with him, but she was a little hesitant to approach him.

CHAPTER SEVENTEEN

Who Served

*G*race

Blaze knelt for her to mount his back. She settled his clothes and grabbed onto his horns as he had instructed. Grace left her stomach behind when he stepped straight into the sky. Once again, she'd given him her fear, and he offered her his strength.

They flew. The wind fluffed her hair behind her as they soared high into the sky. It felt as if they floated in the air as he glided along on a thermal. They skimmed the treetops at unbelievable speeds and flew through clouds.

They dipped low over a pond, and he tilted sideways to skim the water with his leathery wings. He flipped the water into the sky so they breezed through the shower. Blaze made an eerie trumpeting sound she could only believe was dragon laughter.

Flying with a dragon was unbelievable. She never wished to share him with anyone else. She believed flying was too intimate to share with anyone else.

She was afraid, but she wanted to be his Valkyrie. He'd proven she was his lifemate.

Could she give control of part of her life over to him? Could she trade the fear and take his strength forever? Her thoughts left her conflicted.

Blaze had warned her the magic would see his desire as a need and would force her to accept his sexual dominance. He'd already awed her with his skill. Some things they'd done the day before, she never dreamed of.

He valiantly avoided rough play, but she knew he wanted more from her. If he turned her, the magic would force the situation to get the energy required to fuse their souls.

When they landed, it was time to leave for Draoithe. They raced back to the house to get dressed and rode with Flame and Hannah in the Hummer to Draoithe.

Grace had been excited to see the rituals. Blaze explained what happened to her, as the other dragons did the same for their mates. It was enlightening.

She found herself drawn to the pack submission ceremony. She needed to understand how it would work, so she could take part properly.

There were no sounds, no words, only movements and behaviors. It was like watching a silent movie. Grace even wanted to run with them afterward when they disappeared into the trees.

Blaze had held her back and explained the dynamic of the pack and its singular lack of tolerance to non-members.

Hannah had been as excited by the pageantry as well. She'd taken several steps toward following the pack before Flame caught her and stopped her.

Grace understood the vampire's fervent desire to socialize with the pack. Vampires liked the company of others. They weren't solitary immortals.

The Valkyrie and the dragons walked back down the hill to wait for the pack at the retreat. Luke hoped they would move in next weekend.

The Valkyrie had all gotten more acquainted over the last week. They walked together in a group, carrying on multiple conversations, while the dragons walked along the edge of the group, silent and watchful.

It felt good to gossip and discuss the move to Draoithe. Grace realized why the *Run* was mandatory. Everyone at Draoithe worked.

They were all doing their own thing. Even if they worked with other people, it was easy to miss speaking with the other members of the pack.

Even for the non-shifters, socializing afterward was nice. People caught up, learned about one another, and networked.

Somehow, all the women from the warehouse had nothing of their previous lives to return to. The solitary life they had all once led was no longer safe. Draoithe had become the only option available to them. The dragons protected them.

The pack helped them redefine themselves. Luke had made it irresistible for them not to stay. They slowly healed. They had hope. Things would never be the same and they all had scars no one could see, but Grace had Blaze.

Flame tossed Blaze the keys and ran into the trees to fly back with Hannah. When they returned and bid everyone good night, it was after midnight. Grace remained wide awake. She watched her dragon undress for bed.

Blaze was methodical about everything he did. He had the amazing habit of putting things where they belonged. His shoes were on the floor next to his wardrobe. He tossed his shirt and slacks in the hamper on the opposite side, along with his undershirt, boxers, and socks. He hung his belt back in the wardrobe and closed the doors.

What kind of work had he done as a dragon so long ago as the dungeon master had led to such a level of precise order?

Grace had undressed and took a nightdress out of the chest when he touched her. She hadn't thought about any naughty things, nor had she specifically asked him for anything. He caressed her bare shoulders.

Did he see her naked and think she asked him for sex? Where was the line? Still, she aroused him.

She could feel his hard body pressed firmly against her back. He kissed the top of her head, leaving her acutely aware of the size difference between them. If he wanted, he could take from her whatever he desired.

Even with her magic working as it should, he was far more powerful than she was. He did nothing she could call overtly leading. He stroked her arms.

His masculine alpha dominance pressed on her. It wanted her to submit. Blaze would never force her, but when he allowed his alpha nature to show, he walked along a thin line.

His honor wouldn't allow him to force her to do anything she didn't want to do. If she submitted to his alpha authority, however, then he would certainly get what he wanted, and he wouldn't feel guilty.

What he wanted was Grace. He couldn't ask her. He was a dragon who served.

CHAPTER EIGHTEEN

As He Had Said

Grace

That was it! Grace understood. Blaze had a dark side. He had some sexual hangups. He probably didn't even recognize it as odd for an overtly masculine, alpha male not to request her to kiss him or start any kind of sexual activity.

What had he said? *'You will come to me.'*

Oh, he was as kinky as any man, and he had serious skills. Although he would always dominate her, he would also always need her to bring her desire to him.

As long as she submitted, she would remain more than satisfied. If she didn't, he would never ask. He relied entirely on proving his lovemaking skills to the degree she would indeed always desire him.

Grace thrilled at the power she suddenly seemed to have. Blaze felt her desire rise in the link between them. He bent his head to kiss down her neck to her shoulder.

She felt his tongue pressed against her pulse point in time with her heartbeat. He wanted to bite her. She had given him her fear, and he had taken a dominant role.

Without understanding exactly how it happened, Grace had submitted to him completely this time. He would take her as he had never had before.

She wouldn't stop him. She had secretly wanted to submit earlier after they'd flown. He could feel her total surrender through the link.

Blaze turned her body so he could look at her face. She gave over her control then. She wanted his mastery. No one had ever made her feel as Blaze did.

Grace no longer wanted control. If Blaze took her, she could handle it. He was the right man, the only man for that place in her life.

None of her other relationships had ever worked. None of the other men she'd ever been with had ever handled her as Blaze did. She'd never known the pure control a submissive lover could have over a man.

Blaze would provide for all of her needs. He'd protect her and care for her. There would be no more men using her for her magic, nor any more warehouses. She could have her life back better than it had been before.

Blaze would have his freedom, she'd have his magic, and she could drown in his love. She wouldn't have to be afraid anymore. He would never hurt her, only love her.

He would give her his strength if she could love him enough to trust him. She submitted to her alpha male. Grace gave him her heart, and she took his soul.

"Please."

It was all he needed to hear. Blaze bit her, and he caught her in his arms as the pain raced through her. Her body trembled. The saliva from a dragon's bite was painful. She saw the black edges of unconsciousness.

Blaze pulled her blood through the wound on her neck and drank it down. The resulting euphoria was unreal. She almost believed she'd imagined it. How could the bite hurt so much, and the bleeding feel so fantastic? If he drank her dry, she didn't want it to stop.

Blaze used his claw to slice open his neck. Grace feared drinking from him. His magic, like her own, was in his blood, but he was dark. It shouldn't work. But she submitted to him. He helped her shift her position and held her up off the floor so she could reach his neck.

Blaze tasted like the finest *juniper-scented whiskey*. It went down smooth and left her throat on fire, but she drank until the wound sealed itself. Blaze let her body slide down one inch at a time, so her toes touched the floor. He let the friction from her body ease the ache of his erection.

Grace sank to her knees in front of him. He gripped her hair in one hand to stop her. Blaze cut his finger and touched himself. Grace took from him what she wanted and gave him what he needed.

Her hands slid over his thighs, and around his hips, to grip his ass cheeks. She pulled him closer to her, licking her lips. His body trembled in anticipation.

She let her lips slide over the top of his cock and close around the head as her tongue slid over the slit at the top. He groaned in pleasure, loud and long as she tasted him completely differently than before. He was a salty-flavored *juniper and whiskey*.

Grace didn't want to stop. Blaze withdrew from her deliberately. He put another drop of blood on himself. Once again, she licked it off as his member slid over her tongue and back into her mouth. Blaze moaned as he allowed her to lick and suck him over and over.

When he withdrew from her the next time, Grace mewled at him, before she reluctantly let him put the third drop of his blood on himself. He gave in to her desire to pleasure him orally.

She brought him to a climax. He deliberately held her head on him so she would swallow him down. She wanted it.

Grace felt the sedr magic wrap around them and link them together. She was in the lock, and he had the master key.

Blaze gave her the protection she wanted. No other man would ever use her mouth as he'd done. He shielded her from all but himself.

Grace had only read about it. It used the veritas magic he commanded as a dragon shifter. Blaze was over six centuries old. The necromancer who'd made him had been highly skilled. Blaze had command of three different intertwined magics. He had learned how to use it all.

Grace caught her breath. There was a law of three in sedr magic. Nine, being the third multiple of three, was often used to bind things.

Blaze didn't intend to claim his life mate. He intended to take her as his bound and locked dragon consort. He wanted to give her more power than she'd ever known. Her fear rose, but she drank his blood.

Blaze used the link to take her fear from her. She feared what he did, what she'd submitted to, but Blaze held her fear away from her. In its place was immense strength.

"We traded, remember? You submitted. Trust me."

Blaze drew her up from her knees.

Grace went willingly with him to bed. The magic allowed nothing else. Blaze laid her gently on the bed. He spread her legs and lowered his face to her mound. He licked her clit and tasted her honey.

Grace arched into him repeatedly and uncontrollably. Her hands tightened in the top of his hair as he rapidly brought her to a hard, shattering climax.

Grace cried out as the shifter mate bonding magic forced the binding of her soul with his. It needed more energy, but the process had begun. Pain seared through her mind.

Blaze cut his finger and slowly inserted it into her asshole while she writhed in pain. He fingered her ass. He withdrew his finger, squeezed another drop of blood, and reinserted it inside her.

He fingered her ass long and deeply, stretching it for his member. It wouldn't be enough, but he would to take her.

Blaze knelt between her thighs. She shook her head and begged him not to.

He smiled at her. He waited for her to calm down. Blaze was in charge of the situation. The magic would force her to comply with his desires. He wanted her to be his Valkyrie, and he did it, so she was only his.

Blaze used his claw to cut his right palm, and he wrapped his hand around his cock. Covered in his blood, he positioned himself at her anal opening.

"Scream for me, Jewel, and beg me for it."

Blaze slid his slick member into her.

Grace screamed. His cock was too large. It filled her, tearing her. She knew his blood mixed with hers.

His thumb began slowly rubbing her clitoris in a circular motion. His cock felt good filling her up after a few minutes.

She writhed on it, and he slid it in and out of her. She wanted it. Grace begged him for it, as he had said she would.

CHAPTER NINETEEN

Juniper And Whiskey

Grace

"Please, Blaze, Please!"

She screamed his name as he made her come, then emptied his balls into her cavity.

He kissed her slowly as his cock slid out of her. The sedr magic wrapped around them again. Her master key locked her once more. No other man would ever use her again as he had.

Blaze cut his palm again and slid his cock into her pussy, all wet with his blood. He withdrew from her before he touched her center. He stroked himself again, recovering himself in dragon blood, and entered her again. When he cut his palm for the third time, she caught her breath.

Instead of entering her as she had anticipated, he laid down on his back and waited. She looked at him. He smiled at her, but he didn't speak.

If she wanted him, she would have to ride him. She moved over him and sank slowly onto him. He gave her his magic as the dragon flames consumed them both.

When he touched her center, the wings of the Valkyrie opened up and unfurled around her. Her feathers were soft and light cream colored almost the same color as her hair shaped light butterfly wings. The bottom edge flight feathers faded softly to a blue-black color on silver shafts.

Grace extended her wings, stretching them. Then she hooded them both beneath her wings as she rode her dragon.

She rode him hard. The magic pushed her for the energy necessary for the bond to finish fusing their souls. He didn't resist her. He let her ride him as she desired.

When she tired, he gripped her hips to guide her and help her maintain her speed. She felt his cock get harder, then his balls drew up. Grace reached her limit. She writhed around on his cock, lost to her climax as he emptied himself deep inside her.

As his shaft shrank, he let her go, and she slipped off of him, breathing hard. The third multiple of three constricted around her as Blaze's body seized up in pain. He was her key, but he paid the magic price to bind her as his consort, sealing her to only his body.

When she caught her breath, she felt her fangs drop when she looked at him. She needed to bite him and drink from him.

As his body calmed from the sedr magic's price, Grace sank her fangs into his neck. She felt the sting and burn through the link as she wounded him and marked him.

The venom kept the wound from closing, and she drank her fill with him. She pulled his magic into her in great mouthfuls of his blood.

When she could drink no more, her fangs receded, and the wound closed. She felt him bite her and drink from her in a drunken haze.

She was sore all over. Her skin was tight, and the sedr magic had locked her to her key. All the dragon fires winked out. They lay facing one another, breathing hard. She was exhausted.

Jewel, are you okay?

I'm beyond okay. So far I don't have words. You locked me to you. I didn't realize you intended to do it. I was afraid, but then you gave me your strength. It is as you said. You gave me more than I ever dreamed possible. You're my key and can never lie with another. Your key won't fit any lock but mine.

You wanted to be safe. I never wish to be with another. Many immortals have the ability, but few understand how to make it work. It's antiquated, but so am I. I have to warn you. When you change the guises into your full Valkyrie state, your eyes will turn black. It signals to all others you're both bonded and locked with your dragon. I laid claim to you in exchange for all the treasure I can hoard.

You were serious?

I told you I'd found the treasure above all treasures. I'm a dragon and have no need for money. It was a hoard created for you. If you like, I'll continue to grow it for you. I always want my mate to want for nothing.

Blaze, I don't know what to say. You better handle it for me. It's beyond what I need. I just want you. I love you, Blaze.

I love you, too. Tomorrow we shall need to report you took your wings from me. Will you apply to join the pack with me? You will need to swear fealty first.

Oh, yes. I want to join with you. I need this place and these people almost as much as I need my dragon.

Will you sleep with me? I think for once you've exhausted even your dragon.

Jewel laughed out loud as she snuggled up against his hard chest. He pulled the covers, then locked her into his embrace. Satiated, exhausted happiness flowed between them in their link. She breathed in his scent of *juniper and whiskey* and slept soundly.

Epilogue

*L*uke

Blaze and Jewel found him late Sunday morning drinking tea with Eli in his office. He invited them in, and they sat in the chairs in front of the desk.

"My king, I came to apply to join the Druid pack. My Valkyrie has claimed her wings from me. We wish to swear the oath as well."

Blaze and Jewel smiled.

"Congratulations! Can we see your wings?" Eli asked.

His tiger's curiosity overtook her. Luke smiled at that.

Jewel looked at Blaze, and he nodded at her. She stood up and switched guises. Eli and Luke both breathed in quickly when her eyes turned black. Luke looked back at Blaze.

"What did you do?" Luke demanded.

"I gave my Valkyrie what she desired from me."

Luke had ordered Blaze to follow Jewel's request, but things were strange.

"Blaze, you've alarmed Luke because Grace's eyes turned black. Would you explain, please?"

Eli smiled as she laid her hand on Luke's arm. Blaze looked at Jewel, and she blushed as she nodded.

"Jewel isn't a shifter. She required proof that I could truly protect her from being abused or raped again. I sealed her to myself when I took my lifemate as my locked and bonded consort. I gave her my magic, my strength, to protect her from her fear."

"Did you ask him for that?" Eli asked.

Jewel nodded.

"I traded with him. See, I wanted him for myself, but I was too afraid. I confessed it to him. He promised we would go as slow as I wanted. He offered to take my fear away and give me his strength. Last night, I accepted the trade. Blaze deals with the fear, and I have his strength for all my magic."

"How is it even possible?" Luke asked, stunned.

"I'm a dragon shifter. All shifters have sedr magic woven into their shifter magic. It is how the link and bonding rituals work. If you alter the bonding ritual so it more closely resembles the vampire consort bond and add more veritas magic, it will effectively lock your mate to you. She's the lock, and I'm the key."

Blaze tried not to embarrass both Eli and Jewel with details.

"The two of you can only ever sleep with one another?"

Luke remained incredulous.

"I've had my fill of lying with others. I want only Jewel."

"This way, we're both safe from those who would take advantage of us," Jewel whispered.

Blaze looked up at her. Luke saw it then.

Blaze had thought he gave her what she wanted, but she had used his alpha status in their relationship to give him what he needed, too. Her black eyes had alarmed Luke, but it was quite obvious what they had done was mutual between them.

He watched as Blaze grabbed her and kissed her soundly. When he released her, her cheeks grew rosy from embarrassment, but she seemed happy with his response. It appeared as if Blaze and Jewel had a relationship akin to what Fox shared with Artie.

Luke looked at Eli. He could feel the tiger in her edging to the surface as the smell of *jasmine* slowly filled the room after Blaze kissed Jewel.

It receded. Jewel had mated with Blaze. She was no longer a threat to Eli's territory. Luke almost wished she was.

"The council has decided in favor of allowing all the current dragons in residence to join the pack upon application if their Valkyrie has claimed her wings from him. You will both need to swear fealty first. You can do it Saturday, but you may have to be patient when joining the pack. We will attempt two pack submissions a week as necessary, but it depends on whether I can manage the magic."

Luke struggled with adding the magic when those with great power submitted.

"Thank you, Luke."

Jewel said as she hugged Eli. Blaze clasped right forearms with Luke.

"My king."

Blaze nodded at Eli. He and Jewel left.

"Do you think I'll ever convince these dragons to just call me Luke?"

"Maybe, give them time. Blaze has changed a lot. They'll come around, but try not to be angry with them. I don't think anyone ever treated them like people before. Smoke is the only one of them who accepts Fox as his friend more so than as some sort of formal commander, but he and Fox spent years building respect and reliance on their relationship. Even theirs isn't perfect."

Eli smiled at him.

She was sexy. His tiger was all that mattered at that moment. He wanted to kiss her. Luke did just that and forgot about the strange bond a grey dragon had with his ***Sorceress Valkyrie***.

A Sneak Peek at Dark Curse

Flame

He stood, staring. The man who'd raped her writhed in pain at his feet, forgotten for the moment. He was inconsequential, nothing compared to *her*.

She was a vjestice vampire. Her long red hair matted and tangled around her face.

It was enough to make Flame want to send his anger in plumes of fire at her attacker.

Tied face down to the cot, she was delirious with the thirst, tormented with hunger. Her black eyes widened with fresh fear.

Flame froze, lost in the vision momentarily. Flashbacks of another life tormented him before he banished them, along with his fear. His memories couldn't help her, and she was the only thing which mattered.

Flame kicked the man he'd beaten bloody, then passed judgment on the fool after he'd bitten him. He became a full eunuch in short order with the swipe of a razor-sharp claw and dragon flame.

Flame took his identity along with his magic, and the man swore his oath to serve the Valkyries for eternity. None denied a dragon in performing his duties on the orders of his king.

The man would be the dragonsworn servant to the vampire he'd brutalized for all time. It would never be enough payment for the crimes he'd perpetrated against her, but if it would help her heal, then it was how it would be.

If her servant failed to help her, Flame would give the man to the dawn, hopefully without beating him to death first. He was a sacrifice already, but it was dishonorable to harm someone weaker.

At the moment, his anger was winning the war with his honor. She should never have been so abused.

Flame approached her carefully after ordering her servant to wait. She struggled weakly against the restraints to get away from him. She feared him.

Flame moved slowly and whispered to her.

The last thing he wanted was for her to be afraid of him. Considering what she'd been through, she wouldn't see him as her rescuer immediately. She would likely see him as another male abuser.

She looked at him, wild-eyed. Her fear was clear, although she seemed resigned to her fate as she remained trapped.

He prayed she couldn't run from him. He might never catch her if she bolted. Vampires were fast.

"I wish to assist you. Will you accept my help?"

He couldn't force it on her. They had forced too much on her already. Flame wanted her to see him differently than those who'd harmed her. He needed to gain her trust.

Flame wanted to calm her. He couldn't tell if she had any more wounds or if any broken bones.

If she needed more than to feed, he needed to assess it. They also needed to move swiftly.

The evil which permeated the warehouse should burn away. It made his skin crawl.

She nodded. She would accept help, and he reached around her to cut the restraints away from her wrists and ankles.

A beautiful vampire breathed in deep as if she sniffed in his scent. It felt nice, but he thought it was strange behavior unless she wanted to taste him.

When she was free, and Flame had stepped back to get a blanket to cover her, her fangs had extended. He laid the blanket over her and wondered.

Had she smelled his blood? Did she want to drink from him?

She didn't look as if she suffered from bloodlust. Perhaps the thirst had taken her over the edge, and her control failed her.

He looked at the servant. She could drink from him. Flame would stop her after only a little. Just enough to quiet the thirst, and Flame would hunt for her later.

He brought the servant to her and slit his wrist with his claw and held it to her face. As soon as the smell of blood reached her, she had her fangs deep into her servant's wrist.

Her servant silently tried to pull away, and even though Flame knew the venom burned him, Flame gripped the man meant to serve her needs.

She drank deeply. If he didn't fear the bloodlust, Flame would have allowed her to drink her fill, though it ended in her servant's death.

How long had she gone without feeding? Far too long.

He couldn't allow further harm to her. After two minutes, he forcefully separated the servant's wrist from her fangs. He let the dragon flames seal the servant's wrist injury before he pushed the servant away from her.

Flame watched her. She lay still.

She was still too weak to move much more than her eyes. The vampire lifted one hand to brush the loose strands of hair from her face. She missed and sighed as she allowed her hand to fall back to the cot, too weak to try again.

Flame's fear of the blood lust stopped him from giving her more blood to combat her weakness. It should have helped more than it did. Perhaps there was something else wrong.

"I'm Flame. Will you tell me your name?"

She was Nightshade to him, but he wanted her human name, to hear her speak to him. He wanted to learn about her.

"Hannah O'Keefe."

She whispered it before she closed her eyes. Her voice carried the signature soft, slightly slurred tones of the vampire. It drew him in.

The siren song of the vampire was irresistible. Something about vampires excited him, as no other ever had.

She was from the kingdom of Munster? Wait, that no longer existed. Was it still possible the women of her lineage were *den lasair?*

She had the hair for it and the right last name. It was fitting her family's lion represented deathless courage, as she was now a vampire.

Did she even know of her possible heritage? He studied her aura. The flame was present. Nightshade could command the fire from the well. Did she know?

She was beautiful in the way all true Gaelic Irish women were. Fair skin, made more creamy white by her vampiric state. Freckles sprinkled across her cheeks and the bridge of her nose.

Flame knew she was his mate, but he hadn't been prepared for the level of intensity to which looking upon her stirred his feelings. He'd never felt desire for a woman so keenly as he felt it for the vampire before him.

It couldn't have gotten any more complicated. It didn't matter. She was for him. He would deal with the rest later.

Hannah made it difficult for him to think. She was certainly in no condition to view him as a suitor.

He had to move her out of the vile warehouse he found her in. He needed to finish the mission.

He would have time to figure out what to do when they were safe and far from the evil. Her safety and current physical comfort were all he needed to handle at the moment. That he could manage easily.

He didn't need to know how her skin felt or her hair smelled. But he couldn't stop himself from cataloging it all, anyway.

"I need to carry you from here. I need to get you away to someplace safe and comfortable. Will you permit me to lift you and move you from here?"

She couldn't walk out. He wanted to beg her, but it was inappropriate behavior.

His singular desire to help vampires, especially beautiful red-headed ones, he tamped down. His raging need to help his mate was harder to tame, but the last thing he needed was his brother's scrutiny.

It was bad enough Ash had found him working for the vjestice of an enclave in Romania hunting down rogue vampires there about a hundred years ago. He'd gone to learn and stayed to help them with a minor problem in exchange for knowledge.

Ash never asked, and Flame never explained. He was only glad he'd sent Flare away before Ash caught up with him.

"Please, just don't let them find me," she pleaded.

She had that soft drawl heard in vampire speech when it accompanied the vampire allure. But she wasn't actively drawing him in. Still, she was beyond sexy.

Who were *they*? Who was she hoping to avoid? Who chased after his treasure?

Flame felt his anger rising. None would take her from him! She was his treasure. He found her. Only a fool attempted to steal from a dragon.

"Who looks for you?"

He had to ask.

Flame needed to know if there was a threat to her. He would eliminate any threats to her. She should have his protection at all costs. Dying would be worth it, so long as she remained safe.

"The ones like you."

What did she mean, like himself? Did she mean other dragons? Was she concerned about his brothers? It made little sense.

Did she know other dragons? Did she even know he was a dragon? How? Why would she be afraid of them if she knew them? Too many questions for later.

He gently turned her body, wrapped the blanket around her, and lifted her into his arms. She weighed nothing, further angering him.

He settled her head against his chest, and his biceps, so she couldn't fall. Flame met up with his brothers, Luke, and Javier.

When they were all ready, Luke gave the orders, and they left the warehouse burning behind them. The evil burned away.

Want More From The Dream?

That you have read one of my stories is humbling to me. I sincerely hope you enjoyed your experience in the dream. Please be kind and leave an independent author an honest review. Your words about my stories help other readers decide to read in the dream as well and support the creative efforts of one self-publishing tiger. Thank you, -OK

Magic Scroll

Join the **Newsletter** for Behind-the Scenes Updates, Exclusive Offers, Sneak Peeks, and Free Stories!

Please Safelist **opheliakee@opheliakee.com**

Newsletter Friends

OPHELIA KEE

Support an independent author and subscribe to **Read the Draoithe Saga** and read it all before the books publish, while I write and edit, and get all the extras, such as AI audio, character art, lexicons, graphics, videos, and more.

Read the Draoithe Saga

Visit **OpheliaKee.com** for books, audiobooks, e-boxed sets, blog posts, videos, miniseries, the suggested read order, to join the newsletter, and subscribe to Read the Draoithe Saga.

OpheliaKee.com

Welcome to the dream...

Also by Ophelia Kee

Kingdom Rising
Thread
A Pack Forms
Druid Fox
Big Bad Wolf

Royal Council
Arctic Fox
Vampire Knight
Dream Walker
Vampire Panther
Angry King

SORCERESS VALKYRIE

Valkyrie Riders
Quest for the Valkyries
Raven's Rescue
Lord of Dragons
Nephilim's Claim
Dungeon Master
Sorceress Valkyrie

Shadowed Dreams
Still Waters

Crimson Dragon
Ruler of the Mind

Apocalypse Denied
Synner & Sainte
Devil's Sins
Four Horses
Reaper's Debt

Lyons Gate
Druid Ancestry
Ruined Lion
Ghostly Kingdom
Elysian Fields
A Conversation With Dragons

Mystic Dark Prequel Trilogy
Haunted Echoes
Ruined Hearts
Shattered Souls

Mystic Dark
Grim Dark
Kiss Dark
Dream Dark
Lunar Dark
Nightmare Dark
Soul Dark
Blood Dark
Godless Dark

Gods of the Dream
Unlikely Kings
Lost One
Master of Destiny
Forest Lord

Acknowledgments

Thanks, everyone!

I want to say thanks to my mom for always supporting me.

Thanks to my sister who has always been my first beta reader.

Thanks to my dragon for encouraging a tiger to play with books.

Thanks to my lost wolf, who provided inspiration.

Most of all, thanks to my readers who always ask the hard questions, which means I have to write more stories.

I love you, -OK

Contact Ophelia Kee

ARC READERS WANTED

Drop by and say hello!
*Email the author: **opheliakee69@gmail.com**

*Ophelia Kee on Social Media: Look for me on these sites.

YouTube * Threads * Facebook * Instagram * Pinterest * X

I look forward to hearing from you. Sincerely, -OK

About the Author - Ophelia Kee

Not who everyone thinks she is.
The product of someone's imagination.
The end result of a lifetime wishing to get out.
Do not buy the lie.
If you live in fear, you give up freedom.
Taking the risk and making the leap.
Too much of anything is a bad thing.
Innuendo floating on mist rising above water.
Walk away and leave it all behind.
Telling the story that haunts a fantasy.
Catching a dream.
She does not exist.
-Ophelia Kee

OPHELIA KEE

Ophelia Kee